His eyes drifted slowly over her body

Then Fraser touched her and everything changed.

Just the lightest brush of his fingers as he took her empty coffee cup, a small enough contact but capable of filling her body with sheet-fire sensation.

"Yes, I know," he responded huskily to the small ragged gasp she couldn't disguise, his grey eyes narrowed and gleaming as they held hers. "I know," he repeated, acknowledging the reaction that had so shaken her, as if he had experienced it himself. And she watched with wide golden eyes as he put down the cup he had taken from her, her heart beating far too quickly because she knew he was going to kiss her.

And he did. It was completely inevitable.

True to form, the wretch believed she was a pushover, Quilla reminded herself bitterly. And the game progressed one stage further and she could almost hear the applause.

DIANA HAMILTON creates high-tension conflict that brings new life to traditional romance. Readers find her a welcome addition to Harlequin and look forward to new novels by this talented author.

Books by Diana Hamilton

Don't miss any of our special offers. Write to us at the following address for information on our newest releases.

Harlequin Reader Service
P.O. Box 1397, Buffalo, NY 14240
Canadian address: P.O. Box 603,
Fort Erie, Ont. L2A 5X3

DIANA HAMILTON

Games for Sophisticates

Harlequin Books

TORONTO • NEW YORK • LONDON
AMSTERDAM • PARIS • SYDNEY • HAMBURG
STOCKHOLM • ATHENS • TOKYO • MILAN
MADRID • WARSAW • BUDAPEST • AUCKLAND

Harlequin Presents first edition April 1993
ISBN 0-373-11548-2

Original hardcover edition published in 1991
by Mills & Boon Limited

GAMES FOR SOPHISTICATES

CHAPTER ONE

'YOU'VE got to help me, Quilla!' Jon sat forward on the edge of the sofa, his hands gripping the glass in which only a small amount of the generous measure of Scotch she'd given him was left.

They were both pale-skinned but tonight he looked haggard, at least a decade older than his thirty years.

'What else are sisters for?' She spoke lightly, but her amber eyes darkened with concern. She'd been worried about him for some time now. For months he'd appeared to be living on his nerves. 'Tell me about it,' she prompted, watching his throat muscles ripple as he emptied his glass. 'Is it the business?'

Kent Construction, along with Marshbrook, the Richmond house, had been their joint inheritance from a father who had never seemed to care whether either of them lived or died, an inheritance which Quilla had distanced herself from as gracefully as possible. For the last six years Jon had put his whole life into the business, but maybe there were problems that she, as a sleeping partner, should know of.

Perhaps, she thought guiltily, she had been selfish when she'd abnegated all responsibility, choosing to go her own way. But her brother shook his head impatiently, his hazel eyes dark.

'I wish it was that simple. Business problems I can cope with.' He held out his empty glass. 'Give me another of those.'

'Should you, if you're driving?' She was openly frowning now, anxiety making her voice unnaturally sharp. Ever since their mother had been drowned while they'd been on holiday in Cornwall when Quilla had been eight and Jon fourteen, they'd been very close, closer than most brothers and sisters because after the tragedy their father had seemed to prefer to forget their existence.

Jon had always taken care of her and she felt bad now, because she had suspected that something was troubling him and hadn't tried to discover what it was.

He pushed the empty glass over the polished rosewood coffee-table that separated the two facing sofas, his hand shaking, his voice roughening as he told her, 'I came by taxi and I'm spending the night at my club. I've got a working breakfast with Fraser McGill.'

'In that case . . .' Quilla unfolded her long, jeans-clad legs from beneath her and went to pour more Scotch. One for herself, too. She had the feeling she was going to need it. Marian wouldn't be very happy, spending yet another night alone in the huge Richmond house, she reflected wryly. Jon's wife had often complained that he spent more time away on business than he did at home.

Putting both glasses down on the table, she met his eyes, and he said bluntly, 'Marian's having an affair with McGill.'

Marian? Never! Quilla sat down heavily, pushing her long silky black hair back off her face, her eyes incredulous. She simply couldn't believe it.

She had never been able to get close to her sister-in-law, but she would have staked her life on her fidelity. Marian, intense and quiet, had always given the impression of being head over heels in love with her handsome, successful husband. They had always seemed the perfect couple.

'Surely not,' Quilla said sturdily, only to have her confidence shaken when Jon told her tightly,

'I know what I'm talking about, for God's sake! She's been acting strangely for twelve months now.'

'How strangely?' Despite his vehemence, she still couldn't believe what he was saying.

'Weepy—withdrawn——' He shrugged, spreading his hands. 'At first I thought she was overdoing things. Being McGill's PA isn't a doddle, but when I suggested she packed the job in she practically bit my head off. It isn't as if we need the money she earns—but she said her work was the only thing that kept her sane.' His face darkened. 'What she really meant was that if she didn't see McGill she'd go insane.'

Quilla shook her head. 'I'm sure you're wrong.' Fraser McGill had a taste for women, but the brand he favoured came with a sparkle, glamorously packaged. Marian, with her quiet, withdrawn personality, her pleasant face and slightly plump body, her neat and sensible mode of dressing, didn't come anywhere near that category. She was efficient and highly intelligent, otherwise she wouldn't have achieved her present position; too intelligent to wreck her marriage by embarking on an affair with a man who reputedly used women as disposables.

'I wish to God I were.'

Jon had finished his drink and got up to pour himself another, his shoulders bowed, and Quilla, hurting because the brother who meant so much to her was in mental pain, suggested quickly, 'Then tell me what makes you so sure.'

'He's a handsome bastard with a reputation that would make any self-respecting woman run a mile, and about three months ago she started staying late at the office, working with McGill on some hush-hush investment plan. I didn't think much of it to begin with—except that maybe she was trying to get back at me for spending time away on business. But I needed to contact her on one occasion—I'd been called up north in a hurry, a crisis had developed on a shopping-mall project in Glasgow we were involved in—but there was no one there. I got the night security officer; he told me there was no one in the building. So I hung around, thinking she hadn't had to work as long as she'd expected and would walk in at any moment. She walked in two hours later. She looked furtive, yet excited—it's hard to explain. And when I asked how her evening had gone she lied, said she and McGill had been working until an hour ago, he'd driven her home, but had declined her offer of coffee. After that I checked up on her every time she said she was working late. There was never anyone there.'

He gulped down his third whisky and pulled a face. 'A fortnight ago I began preliminary discussions with McGill over funding for a new development scheme. We had lunch. I had these suspicions but couldn't be sure Marian hadn't used the working-late-at-the-office excuse as a cover for seeing some other guy. So over coffee I asked him how much longer he was going to expect my wife to work long hours of overtime, making a joke of it. And for the first time ever I saw Fraser McGill lose that damned urbanity of his. He looked guilty as hell, said something like, "Not for too much longer, I hope," and changed the subject. I felt like murdering him.'

'Have you told her you know what's going on?' Quilla asked thinly, her eyes dark with compassion and shock. She couldn't believe Marian would be unfaithful, and Jon shook his head, slumping back opposite her, his eyes bleak.

'I was too afraid to. I don't want to lose her. If I came out and accused her she'd walk out for good. Things haven't been going well for us for some time—well before her affair with McGill started. She wants a family, and started getting uptight because nothing happened. I told her it didn't matter to me. That's when things began to go wrong.' He sighed raggedly. 'Sure, I'd like kids, too, but I wouldn't feel cheated if we didn't have any. Marian's all I want.'

'Did you tell her that?' Quilla questioned, and Jon shook his head tiredly.

'I didn't think I needed to.'

'Then you should,' she said, exasperated, her heart wrenching as she remembered how it had felt, as a child, not to be particularly wanted.

Her father had idolised her mother and, after her death, he had turned his back on his children, perhaps resenting the fact that they still lived when the wife he'd adored had gone. Jon seemed to be following his father's pattern, not realising it, as far as the woman in his life was concerned. And if he hadn't fully explained how he felt then Marian could hardly be blamed for believing that, if not having children together didn't matter to him, then she didn't, either.

'And there's worse,' Jon said, his voice heavy. 'The weekend after next, so she tells me, she's going to visit some old school friend I've never before heard her mention. Apparently, she lives in some remote Welsh village, and I offered to drive her there, but she wouldn't hear of it. She'll be spending the weekend with McGill, that's obvious. That's where I need your help.'

He stood up, pacing the room edgily, and Quilla said quickly, 'I'll do anything I can.' If he wanted her to talk to Marian, she would, but she didn't think it would do much good. There had never been any open animosity between them but Quilla had always felt that Marian resented the deep bond between herself and Jon.

'When's Nico due back?' Jon asked abruptly, his eyes scanning the large sitting-room, the modern uncluttered furnishings, as if he expected his sister's partner to appear in a puff of blue smoke.

'Not until tomorrow. He's in Rome, ordering fabrics.'

He relaxed fractionally, but his face was grey as he turned to her.

'We're having a business meeting at Marshbrook this weekend. Lionel Crane will be there—he's the developer I'm partnering in the project I told you about, a luxury hotel and sports complex on the south coast—and Emma, his wife. And McGill.' His voice hardened. 'We're hoping Rowan, McGill and Cade will fund the project. Primarily, of course, it's business. But we're starting out with dinner on Friday night followed by discussions after breakfast the next morning. Then lunch. I want you there for the social side of it. No one will think it odd—you're my sister and you'll make up the numbers in what will be as much a social weekend as a business affair. Will you come?'

'Of course, if you want me to.'

She rarely went to Marshbrook now, feeling that Marian was uneasy about her own part ownership of the house. And she didn't see how her presence would help Jon's problem and was horrified when he enlightened her.

'I want you to make a heavy play for McGill.'

'A what?' Quilla yelped when his words finally sank in, not wanting to trust her own hearing. 'You can't be serious. I don't even know the man!'

'I've never been more serious, sis,' he stated heavily. 'It's the only solution I can think of, and you're the only one I could ask. You're his type— beautiful, glossy, sophisticated. If you show him you're interested he'll respond and he won't suspect a thing—his ego's too damned big to let him. And if Marian sees him in his true colours—a woman-ising bastard who can't keep his hands off any attractive, willing woman who offers—she'll drop him like a hot brick. Because, despite what's happened, she's got integrity and she is fastidious. She'll be hurt for a time, but she'll get over it.' His eyes blazed suddenly. 'She's damned well got to! And when she does come to her senses she'll realise the love I can offer is worth a hell of a lot more than a no-hope affair with that swine.'

'And if she doesn't?' Quilla asked unsteadily, appalled by what he was asking her to do.

'Then I'll divorce her,' he stated flatly. 'I blame him more than I blame her, and if she drops him I'm willing to forget it ever happened. But I can't go on like this. Say you'll do it?'

Quilla stared at him wide-eyed, her heart thumping. She didn't see herself as a siren, irresistible, certainly not to a man as experienced as McGill was reputed to be. And the thought of deliberately setting out to offer herself to a man, then refusing to deliver, made her feel ill.

'It would only need to be for the weekend,' Jon implored. 'As soon as Marian sees how quickly he jumps at any likely offer she'll be off him for life. Then you can tell him to go boil his head.'

'I can see that doing your business deal a whole heap of good,' she scorned, but he was in there quickly.

'He wouldn't let a sexual put-down affect his business judgement. That, at least, is as sound as a bell. And I very much doubt if he knows that Father left the company between the two of us. You take no part in it, don't even claim your share of the profits. As far as he's concerned you'll simply be there to make up the numbers.'

Despite her distaste for the whole awful idea, Quilla could see his logic. If he wasn't prepared to tackle Marian head on, and risk her walking out on him for good, going to her lover, then showing McGill up for the rake he was, disillusioning her utterly, was a way of ending the whole sordid affair with the least harm done.

That was Jon's way of looking at the situation. She wasn't at all sure she agreed with it but if nothing was done and the marriage ended in divorce then Jon would spend the rest of his life being unhappy. Like his father, he was a one-woman man; he would end up bitter and lonely and, like their father, work himself into an early grave because he saw nothing else to do with his life.

Jon had always done so much for her—she couldn't have had a more caring brother. After the death of their mother he had seemed the only person to show any real affection. Their father's uninterest had brought them closer together.

It was time she repaid her debt, though the method of repayment was not one she was happy with.

'I ordered oceans of the most wickedly delicious fabrics you've ever clapped eyes on!' Nico walked into the kitchen the following day as Quilla was chopping salad stuffs to go with the omelette she had planned for supper. 'The bill will make even your hair curl!'

Quilla smiled for the first time since Jon had left the previous evening. The dead straightness of her long black hair was a standing joke.

It was good to see him. He looked as fresh as a daisy after what must have been a gruelling three days in Rome visiting fabric showrooms and warehouses. His deep golden tan contrasted dramatically with his lint-blond hair, and the white shirt he was wearing. With his unusual colouring he cultivated flamboyance, wearing it like a second skin. It made good publicity, and in the fashion game the style of the designer was almost as important as the style of his products.

Four years ago she had met Nico French at a party. At the time she had been working in an advertising agency as a very junior part of the copywriting team, and Nico had been a fledgeling designer, determined to go to the top.

Although there had never been anything sexual in their relationship, they had taken to each other on sight, and three months later they had become a team, pooling their financial resources and talents.

'You don't apologise for your garments,' she had ordered sternly. 'You go right out there and tell buyers how privileged they are to be invited to stock your label!'

Between them they had bought a large Victorian house in Southwark, the still unfashionable quarter of London's Docklands, converted a room for Nico's studio and another, smaller one for Quilla's office. The next step was to lease a disused warehouse near the Rotherhithe Tunnel for a workroom and storage space.

While Nico concentrated on his designs, supervised their small team of pattern cutters and machinists, Quilla concentrated on letting the world know that the Nico French label was worth its weight in gold.

And she had succeeded, blatantly courting the fashion editors of the glossies, persuading the owners of prestigious boutiques throughout the UK and Europe to feel honoured because they were allowed to stock Nico's creations, organising discreetly luxurious shows in top flight hotels in every major city, making sure that an invitation to a Nico French evening was prized beyond rubies. Quality not quantity was their aim, exclusivity above all else.

'Are you cooking for me?' Nico enquired with a lilt of one blond eyebrow, and Quilla grinned.

'If you'll make do with an omelette, yes. If you want something more exotic you'll have to fend for yourself. And by the way, I've booked the venues and models for the spring show,' she went on. 'London, Birmingham, Edinburgh, Paris, Rome...'

The bi-annual travelling circus encompassed three weeks of frenetic activity. Quilla both loved and loathed it, but she would prefer to have a tooth pulled than miss a single moment.

'Great.' Nico reached into the fridge for a bottle of wine, adding, with the perspicacity that would have surprised the many who thought him a lightweight, a talented butterfly with no thoughts in his head beyond the vagaries of fashion, 'Is that why you're wearing bags under your eyes today? Or is it a trend I've missed? No problem with the shows?'

Quilla shook her head, smiling. She supposed she was looking bleary-eyed. She'd lain awake half last night worrying about the seemingly precarious state of her brother's marriage, about the prospect of the coming weekend.

Bags under her eyes! Nico could insult a girl in the nicest way! Sometimes she thought he didn't like women, or couldn't trust them. She had never asked. Firm friends though they were, there were some areas in their respective lives where neither pried.

'No, no problem with the shows.' She tipped the egg mix carefully into the omelette pan while he hunted down the corkscrew. 'I've been summoned to a weekend houseparty at Marshbrook, and I'm not looking forward to it,' she said, deliberately understating the deep distaste she felt for the part she would be expected to play.

Nico shot her an astute blue look, asking, 'Who'll be there? Anyone exciting?'

'Not so you'd notice.' Quilla added mushrooms to the pan and deftly flipped the omelette over, adding, her offhandedness a contrivance only she knew how difficult it was to achieve, 'The Cranes, business associates of Jon's, and Fraser McGill.'

'Oh, mucho macho!' Nico made a flourish with the bottle of wine, hiding his far too handsome face behind his free hand, camping it up outrageously. 'Pack your chastity belt, dear one, do! From what the little birds all tell me, no woman really wants to be safe when he's around, but you're far too individual to join any queue.'

'And if I wanted to—join the queue?' She manufactured a teasing smile, testing the water as she divided the omelette between two plates. Nico knew everyone, all the gossip; he made it his business, and she knew him well enough not to be disconcerted when he replied with the thoughtful seriousness which, when he wasn't putting on an act, revealed his true nature,

'If you were brave—or foolish—enough to do any such thing, he'd take one look at you and make damn sure you leapt right to the head of it.'

Which would make her task much easier, Quilla decided two days later as she drove out of London, heading for Richmond. Or more difficult, depending on the way it was viewed, she thought hollowly.

As the weekend had rushed nearer, her promise to help her brother had been regretted more than once. She got butterflies in her stomach every time she thought about what she had agreed to do.

It wasn't the thought of leading McGill on then dropping him flat that bothered her. From all accounts a put-down of that nature was long overdue. It might even be good for his soul to discover that he wasn't as irresistible as he reputedly believed he was!

No, it was the idea of publicly acting out the vamp-like role assigned to her. It would have to be very public, otherwise the exercise would be pointless. Everyone, Marian in particular, must be made to believe that she was blatantly offering herself to McGill and that he was grabbing with both hands!

The thought of acting so much out of character, in such an outrageously sexual manner, was deeply distasteful.

Wrinkling her forehead, she tried to collate all the information she had gleaned about the man she had reluctantly come to think of as her prey. Such information as she had was only superficial, of course, garnered from hearsay, from articles in the financial press and gossip columns, but it might help.

That he was rarely seen, socially, without a beautiful woman on his arm was well known, and she glossed over that fact, bringing her concentration to bear on what she had learned about the other side of his character.

About his early life she knew nothing, but now, at around the age of thirty-five, he was chairman of Rowan, McGill and Cade, self-styled dictator of his own financial kingdom. Eight years ago, apparently, he had been co-opted as trouble-shooter for the then moribund, long-established merchant bankers Rowan Cade. And after the dust of the upheaval he had instigated had settled he had emerged as chief executive. From then on it had been only a matter of time before the bank had become a powerful force in the financial markets of the world, and Fraser McGill the uncrowned king in the dog-eat-dog world of high finance. He was ruthless, pushy and, to help her brother, she was about to use herself as bait in the oldest trap in the world!

'You're in your old room; you know the way.' Marian's tone implied that she resented the fact, and Quilla wished she had taken the trouble to get to know her sister-in-law much better. If she had, then maybe a serious talk, a friendly word of warning, would have sufficed, obviating the need for the distasteful role Jon expected her to play this weekend.

But she had tried, Quilla thought a shade wildly as she returned the stiff smile Marian had greeted her with. She'd tried hard to penetrate the other woman's reserve at first. But Jon hadn't helped, she remembered ruefully, always insisting on consulting her, as joint owner of Marshbrook, on anything from the addition of the conservatory to the choice of new wallpapers, impressing on his bride that the house he had brought her to was as much Quilla's as hers, her decisions on re-modelling it as likely to be overturned as not.

Not that Quilla had ever done any such thing. She would never dream of vetoing any suggestion of Marian's. As far as she was concerned, Marshbrook belonged to her brother and his wife and, if the outcome of this weekend's charade was satisfactory, she would deed her share in the house to Marian. She should have done it years ago.

'Of course. Thank you—but, before I go up, is there anything I can do to help?'

Quilla injected warmth into her tone but was met by a blank stare, a brief, dismissive, 'No, nothing. I am capable of running a social weekend on my own.'

'Of course you are,' Quilla replied, sighing, watching her sister-in-law hurry away towards the rear of the hall. Once again, she had her doubts about Marian's supposed affair with McGill. With the best will in the world, not even her closest friend would describe Marian as beautiful or glitzy—and, according to rumour, McGill demanded both qualities from his women.

It was a thought she hung on to determinedly as she made her way up the broad polished staircase and along the thickly carpeted corridor to her old room. Maybe Jon had got his wires crossed on this. That Marian had lied about working late wasn't in dispute. But having an affair with her boss? It simply didn't hold water. So, she comforted herself, no need to hurl herself into the fray; she would first observe them together, draw her own conclusions before she put herself on the line.

She was still thinking along these hopeful lines when she emerged from the shower-room adjoining her bedroom, clad in a robe while she deliberated on what to wear for the evening ahead.

Leaving her options open, she had packed a demure black cocktail dress as well as a far more glamorous number to go with her distasteful *femme fatale* role.

Following a brief tap on the door, Jon edged quietly into the room. He was already dressed for dinner and his face was strained, and Quilla told him grumpily, because she wasn't in the best of moods, 'If you ask me if it's OK by me if you go ahead and get the chimneys re-pointed, or change the dining-room curtains—in front of poor Marian—one more time, I'll scream! It's no wonder she resents me.' She sat down at the dressing-table and began dragging a brush through her long black hair, her normally pale face burning. Despite four years of marriage Jon knew nothing about women, and if Marian was straying it could be largely his fault!

'It's as much your house as mine,' Jon objected, bewildered by her outburst. 'Why shouldn't you be consulted about it? And Marian doesn't resent you, why on earth should she?' He had gone to sit on the end of the bed, his hazel eyes holding her stormy golden ones in the mirror.

'Because, for one thing, you make her feel that I have more say in what goes on here than she does herself. Think about it.' She swiped the brush through her hair savagely. 'And when you've got your marriage sorted out I'm making my share in the house over to her. I should have done it years ago.'

'I can't let you do that,' he said stiffly, pulling himself to his feet.

Quilla flung the brush down, making the cut glass toiletries clatter, grating, 'So you can't let me make a simple move like that—one that couldn't possibly hurt me and yet would do Marian, and quite possibly your marriage, a power of good, and yet you'll happily ask me to put my head in the lion's mouth!'

'You've changed your mind,' he stated bleakly. 'I came to tell you—McGill arrived just after the Cranes, about ten minutes ago. He's in his room, changing for dinner.'

'Oh, great!' Quilla's nerves were at screaming pitch, the thought of what Jon was expecting her to do making her feel ill. 'What do you want me to do?' she snapped. 'Run to his room and rape him?'

'If you're in that sort of mood——' He clamped his mouth shut, walking to the door, leaving her to get her temper under control. She knew how much he loved his wife, and how little he understood the mistakes he had made. But even if he wasn't the most sensitive and understanding husband in the world he was the best brother any girl could have.

She knew that the despair on his face as he'd walked out of the room would haunt her. She owed him so much and she knew she had to reassure him, tell him she would do as he'd asked. At least, she amended silently as she hurried to the door, intending to call him back, she would do it if she believed it would serve any useful purpose.

Observing Marian and McGill together this evening should tell her all she needed to know. When a woman was with the man she loved she couldn't hide her feelings.

Opening the bedroom door, she sagged back defeatedly against the frame. The corridor was empty. Guilt made her chew impatiently on her wide lower lip. Jon had to be feeling wretched enough without her mean-minded display of sarcastic temper.

So she'd just have to dress in record time, rush downstairs and find her brother before any of the others put in an appearance, give him all the reassurance he needed. She was on his side, after all.

As she turned back to her room, her movements were arrested when a door further along the corridor opened. Marian emerged, followed by a man who could only be McGill. She was dressed for dinner, in a crêpey dress in one of the neutral shades she favoured, but he was naked, apart from a towel slung precariously low on his hips.

Quilla held her breath, her heart pounding like a steam hammer. McGill had his back to her, droplets of water glistering on his dark hair, on the golden skin that covered his arrestingly masculine body. She couldn't see his face, but she could see Marian's. The other woman looked more animated than Quilla had ever seen her before, her cheeks pink, her rosy mouth parted, making her look deliciously pretty, utterly vulnerable, the way only a woman deep in the throes of a powerful infatuation could look.

And one of McGill's hands came up, tilting Marian's chin as he murmured something Quilla was too far away to hear. But she couldn't miss the way Marian's eyes drifted shut, the ecstatic smile on her lips, and she slid back into her room, closing the door very quietly behind her, sickened by the scene she had witnessed.

After a moment, however, she was back in control, her mouth determined. Jon was right, and she was going to have to do as he had asked. She was going to have to make Marian see that, as far as McGill was concerned, she was only a passing amusement, to be callously dropped the moment he scented a new conquest.

Impatiently, she tossed the discreet little black dress aside and reached for the other, ignoring the flutter of nerves in her stomach.

She was embarking on a game for sophisticates and she didn't know the rules.

But that didn't mean she wasn't going to win!

CHAPTER TWO

THE conversation stopped as Quilla walked into the room. She had deliberately taken her time, electing to make an entrance.

There weren't many people in the elegantly furnished drawing-room, of course. Just five. Five pairs of eyes absorbing the impact she made.

The sleeveless gold tissue dress was one of Nico's; she had worn it last winter for the press launch of this season's collection. The neckline dipped deeply at the back and front, right down to the tiny waist, the top slightly bloused, giving the erroneous impression that it would reveal all when she moved, the skirt narrow, clipping her hips, ending just above her knees. The design was Nico French at his most elusively sexy, and the impact was stunning.

She turned, making her eyes enigmatic, as Jon touched her elbow, the sheer relief in his eyes making her feel her efforts had been worthwhile. She had left her long hair loose, knowing the innocence of the style contrasted piquantly with both the dress and the make-up she had used to emphasise her long, black-fringed golden eyes, the jawline she considered too wide, and the sensual line of her mouth. She didn't believe it when people said she was beautiful but knew she could, if she tried, make herself look interesting.

And, it seemed, she had succeeded.

23

Jon introduced her. Emma Crane, well into middle age but elegant in deep blue silk, her intelligent eyes busily putting a price tag on the Nico French dress, her husband's eyes imagining what lay beneath the gold fabric.

Deliberately, Quilla refused to allow her dislike of such open appraisal show. She forced a smile to her copper-tinted lips, carefully not looking McGill's way. He was, as yet, simply a dark presence and she turned beneath the gentle pressure of Jon's hand on her waist, glimpsing Marian's tight smile as she approached with a heavy Georgian decanter. Quilla's stomach twisted with pity. If all went as Jon had planned then her sister-in-law would be a very disillusioned lady before the evening was over.

'Quilla, meet Fraser McGill.' Jon's voice was threaded with a note of almost vicious triumph. 'McGill, my sister.'

She had to look at him then, trying to make her smile sultry, even though the effort sickened her. She had chosen to wear the highest heels she owned, gold kid backless sandals that made her elegant legs look endless, but even so he towered above her and the impact of his animal magnetism made her heart kick against her ribs.

His dark craggy features couldn't be called handsome; no vacuous Greek god type this—but all male, virile, tough, the hard aggressive jawline and prominent nose starkly emphasising a wide, utterly sensual mouth.

'Fraser,' she acknowledged, and the huskiness of her voice wasn't manufactured as she slid her fingers into his outstretched hand, deliberately steeling herself to close them around the hard bones with a delicate pressure that went way beyond the mores of polite introduction.

The momentary affliction of her vocal cords was down to sheer terror, she recognised sickly as she slowly veiled her eyes, cutting out the probing scrutiny of his cool, alert, highly intelligent grey assessment.

What on earth was she supposed to do now? she wondered feverishly. Just stand here, like a beast in a cattle market, while his knowing eyes assessed her finer points?

He was lazily undressing her with his eyes, each glance a sensual caress. Her body burned where his eyes touched and she saw Marian move, on the periphery of her vision, and made herself move closer to him, nerves making her voice throaty again as she husked out the first inane comment that came into her head.

'I'm so glad to have met you at last; I've heard so much about you.' She felt her throat close up as she registered the mocking, slightly inquisitorial lift of one black, arched brow.

Thankful for the distraction, she accepted the sherry Marian gave her, sipping it quickly to cover her confusion. It was very dry, the way she liked it, and she'd have to get her act together if she was to make any impression at all on the ruthless bastard who was indulging in a casual affair with her brother's wife.

McGill would be well used to presentable women giving him the obvious green light—they would crawl out of the woodwork in droves when he was around. So far all she had done was arouse cynical amusement in him, and she was going to have to work out some kind of strategy.

But how? All she wanted to do was wring his neck. And Marian's!

Murmuring an excuse, she went to join her brother and Emma Crane, unaware of the seductive sway of her reed-slim body in the shimmering golden dress.

Turning her back on McGill didn't mean she was any the less aware of him. Her skin prickled with tension simply because he was in the same room, breathing the same air.

At dinner she was seated opposite him and for the first time in her life she was utterly tongue-tied. Marian had gone to a great deal of trouble. The elegant silver and crystal on the table, the candles and discreet floral decorations all added the right sophisticated touches, and the food her housekeeper had prepared was perfectly cooked and presented, quite delicious. And yet here she was, the would-be *femme fatale*, feeling and acting like a speechless nervous schoolgirl!

She had had men friends, of course she had, quite a few, but there had never been anything serious in her relationships. One day she would like to fall in love and marry, have a family, but not yet. She enjoyed her freedom and career too much to want anything to change.

And the men she had dated had always sought her out. She had never before deliberately set out to capture any man's interest and, far from engaging McGill in the type of provocative word-play that would let him know she was interested and available, she seemed to have been struck dumb.

But the others more than made up for her lack of sparkle, the chit-chat passing back and forth like glittering ping-pong balls, McGill's contribution to the conversation revealing a dry wit that normally would have appealed to her. And every time she raised her eyes she found his cool grey gaze on her and felt her pulse-beats quicken immediately. And she knew she had failed miserably in her attempts to help her brother because, for once, Marian was sparkling vividly, hanging on McGill's every word, her eyes rarely leaving his face.

Jon, though, seemed to take a different view of the situation. Coming to stand behind her as he circled the table, refilling wine glasses, he leaned forwards, pretending his cuff-link had caught in one of the long, ornate gold drop ear-rings she wore.

'You're doing great,' he murmured, his voice too low for anyone else to hear. 'That sultry, silent siren act is far more intriguing than a load of chatter and innuendoes.'

Giving her an affectionate smile, he filled her glass and moved away. The poor lamb was trying to boost her confidence; he must have realised how gauche she felt! Her lips parted on a compassionate smile and she glanced across the table, wondering if the hateful McGill had noticed the small interchange, and found him, yet again, looking at her, his eyes gleaming wickedly as he tilted his glass towards her in a graceful toast, holding her unwillingly mesmerised gaze as he drank.

She didn't know how she got through the remainder of the meal. If Jon was right and McGill had found her silence intriguing, which that wordless toast and smouldering look had seemed to signify, then what was she going to do about it?

In any case, his interest—if interest it was—was far too subtle. Maybe he would discreetly ask for her phone number before the weekend was over.

One thing she was rapidly finding out was that he was far more subtle than his reputation had led her to believe.

But his discretion wouldn't get her anywhere. The whole object of this unpleasant exercise wasn't to maybe have him following up any vague sexual interest she might have aroused in him this weekend, but to get him to make his lustful intentions clear to Marian!

'I don't know what's come over him!' Marian exclaimed as they at last moved slowly out of the dining-room, leaving Mrs Hodge, the grumpy housekeeper with a heart of gold whose services had been inherited from their father, along with the house, to clear away. 'Jon usually insists on talking business after dinner on occasions like these, leaving the women to kick their heels!'

'It won't take a moment to clear the hall. I always said it would be perfect for dancing,' Jon was saying, striding ahead to move the few Persian rugs that were scattered over the polished parquet, pushing the armchairs closer to the wide stone hearth.

The outer door was open, admitting warm night air, heavy with the scent of honeysuckle, and as the first strains of music came from the stereo Quilla made an unconscious half-turn and found McGill's arms around her.

He had strong arms, she thought bemusedly, her tall body moving fluidly with his to the sensuous beat of the music, and she caught her breath as his hold on her tightened, pulling her closer to the hard length of his body, making every inch of her skin unbearably sensitised.

His physique was as powerful as his intellect, she registered dazedly as her fingertips splayed against the expensive fabric that covered his wide, rangy shoulders. And he was obviously enjoying the close contact. She could feel the electricity of sensual awareness, feel the heat of his thighs as they brushed against hers, and she knew the moment had come to make a move which would force him to display that enjoyment to the others, to Marian in particular.

The thought most definitely did not appeal and she opened eyes which had unwittingly closed and glanced around. Marian was dancing with Lionel Crane, a polite hostess smile on her face. She looks really graceful when she dances, Quilla thought, well aware that her errant sister-in-law would be aching to dance with McGill.

Steeling herself, she waited until Marian couldn't avoid seeing what she was doing, swallowed the acid taste of self disgust and dragged out a deep sigh, winding her arms around McGill's hateful neck and resting her head against his chest, hearing the powerful drum beats of his heart.

The flicker of something indefinable in Marian's eyes gave Quilla a momentary sense of achievement, but it was short-lived and turned to utter panic when McGill took her embrace as an open invitation to trail his mouth over the tip of her silky head, nuzzling aside the wings of dark hair to taste the frantic pulse-beat at her temple.

He was playing the part she had allotted him perfectly, but it was truly awful. Self-loathing was turning her bones to jelly and she couldn't believe she was behaving this way, wantonly pressing her body against that of a man she had not even met until two or three hours ago. A man she had every reason to despise.

Every instinct in her urged her to extricate herself, walk away from him, but she knew she couldn't allow herself that luxury.

Marian had to witness her lover openly respond to the advances of another woman; only then would she see McGill for what he was—a cruelly careless, womanising rat!

And now his hand was moving over her back where the clever, sexy styling of the dress left it bare, the pads of his fingers trailing erotic patterns on her skin. And she simply couldn't bear any more.

'I think it's time you danced with your hostess, don't you?' She made her voice velvet soft, even managed to inject a note of husky regret, because to yell at him to take his foul hands off her most definitely wasn't part of the plan.

'You're probably right.' He released her with every appearance of genuine reluctance, but the grey eyes gleamed, something devilish looking out at her, something that told her he wasn't finished with her yet.

She shuddered violently, walking away. Let him dance with Marian, let her give him a blistering earful for practically making love on the dance-floor with her husband's sister. She hoped his ears would get burned to a cinder!

She shivered with reaction now, with disgust at the games people played, and as Jon relinquished Emma Crane to her husband Quilla grabbed his arm.

'Dance?' He was looking more relaxed than she had seen him look in months and she answered snappily,

'No, thanks. I've just had enough of that particular form of exercise to last for years!'

'Don't knock it.' His mouth quirked. 'You were
fantastic! The bastard hasn't taken his eyes off you
since you made that entrance before dinner. And
Mari's not blind. It's working out the way I figured
it would, so don't give up on me now, there's a
love.'

Quilla's yellow eyes glinted with temper. Jon
might be confident about the outcome of this evening's ghastly charade, but she wasn't. She had
witnessed the revealing scene in the dim corridor
upstairs, and he hadn't. And she couldn't tell him
because she knew how much his wife's infidelity
was hurting him. She couldn't hammer yet another
nail into his heart.

Witnessing that scene had been responsible for
her decision to demean herself and do as he had
asked. But she had done enough self-demeaning to
last more than one lifetime. It left a nasty taste in
her mouth and her flesh still crawled and tingled
from being held so intimately in McGill's arms. She
had had enough, had done enough, and she could
tell him that.

'I'm going to bed. If anyone asks, I've got a
headache. And from now on it's your pigeon—I've
got an aversion to being pawed.' She began to walk
away, her spine rigid. 'I suggest you stop trying to
use me and start beating McGill at his own game.
Make your wife believe she's someone special. Ask
him what the knack is, if you don't already know.'

The sudden bleak anxiety in his eyes haunted her
all the way to her room, but she deliberately
hardened her heart as she stripped off her clothes
and soaped herself vigorously under the shower,

trying to erase the memory of how McGill's hands had made her feel.

The womanising bastard deserved to have his precious ego dented. And if any other woman had set out to do just that she would have applauded her all the way. That she should feel bitterly ashamed of herself for agreeing to what Jon had asked, in an attempt to save his marriage, was a conundrum she couldn't be bothered to solve.

In any case, her mind was made up. She would set her travelling alarm and leave Marshbrook long before the others were stirring in the morning. She had done all she intended to do, all she could stomach, and it was up to Jon to sort out his marriage.

She was going to forget Fraser McGill existed and get on with her highly satisfactory life.

'Have dinner with me tonight.'

There could be no mistaking that deep, slightly abrasive voice, and Quilla felt her face go hot, almost dropping the receiver in a flurry of panic as her eyes darted round her neat office, as if trying to find a way of escape.

'No. I already have a date,' she prevaricated wildly before the silence coming from her end could become too suspect. Two days ago when she'd crept away from Marshbrook in the hazy sunlight of a June dawn she had rejoiced in the sudden feeling of freedom. She had seen and heard the last of Fraser McGill!

How wrong she had been.

'Cancel it.'

'I can't, even if I wanted to.' The tinge of asperity in her voice was a direct response to the lazy thread of amusement in his authoritative tone and her skin crawled hotly as he responded, the dark vibrant voice undeniably sexy.

'You shouldn't start something you've no intention of finishing. I'll pick you up at eight.'

She slammed the phone down at that particular arrogance, her face burning with a mixture of humiliation and rage. What sort of woman did he think she was? No, better not try to answer that, she thought rawly, picking up the phone again, her fingers shaking as she punched the numbers.

'Did you give McGill my number?' she accused waspishly as soon as she was through to Jon.

He answered quickly, 'I had no option. Sorry. He asked me for it in front of Mari, and it was too good an opportunity to miss. She'd already commented on how well the two of you had taken to each other; how the chemistry between you was practically visible—her words, not mine. So him asking for your address and phone number seemed like a godsend, especially as you'd already sloped off.'

'So Marian's seen through him, come to her senses?' Relief flooded sweetly through her. She knew how much her brother loved his wife. The fact that he was willing to forget and forgive her infatuation for McGill, provided it ended, was proof of that. She could only be thankful that the crazy scheme had actually worked...

'It would appear not,' Jon said heavily, wiping the slate clean of the one positive aspect of the whole unpleasant mess. 'She still plans to visit her "friend" next weekend. When I told her to be sure to leave a number where I could contact her if necessary she turned a bright shade of pink and

muttered something about looking it up for me.'
He sighed raggedly. 'I know she intends spending
the weekend with McGill, so if he contacts
you——'

'He already has,' Quilla snapped. If Marian
walked through the door now she would strangle
her for what she was doing to Jon.

'Well, I was wondering,' Jon began weakly.

Quilla snapped right back, 'Wondering what,
precisely?' She knew, oh, yes, she knew, but she
gritted her teeth, waiting for him to get it out.

And he did.

'Well, if he suggests seeing you again, could you
hold him off until the weekend? Say you'll see him
then. If he's with you he can't be with my wife.'

Quilla counted to ten. Slowly. This was her
brother, she reminded herself. The brother who had
given her so much support and affection when she
had needed it most. He had been father, mother
and brother all rolled into one at the time when she
had been grief-stricken by the loss of her mother
and bewildered by the remoteness in her father. It
was something she could never forget, so she
managed to swallow the instinct to tell him to get
lost and said reasonably, 'If you want me to spend
the weekend with him you'd better forget it,' and
heard him explode,

'No, no, no! You're making me sound like a
pimp! You're my little sister, remember?'

'I'm glad you reminded me!' she sniped, only to
hear him elaborate.

'Much as I, personally, would like to see him rot
in hell, the man's not a raving sex maniac. If you
suggested a theatre, say, followed by a late supper
on Saturday evening, that would slice through any

weekend plans he's made that involve Marian. You needn't even turn up. You could invent a sudden attack of flu, or a business crisis. You invented your way out of the weekend at Marshbrook with no trouble at all.'

She deserved that crack, she owned. And what he suggested sounded feasible, to a fool! But she wasn't a fool and she had first-hand knowledge of McGill's unashamed persistence, didn't she? So she said patiently, 'I'm having nothing more to do with this cloak and dagger stuff. You should sit down quietly with Marian, tell her you know about her relationship with McGill and ask her to end it.'

'I'm afraid to, Quilla.' The evident strain in his voice made her frown worriedly. 'I know, deep down, that Mari still loves me, but things have been going wrong for months. It's been like walking on eggshells. I'm to blame, too. I should have taken time to talk to her about our apparent inability to have children. It doesn't matter to me whether we have children or not, because she's all I need. It might matter to her—but now isn't the time to talk seriously to her about anything.' She recognised the pain in his voice and could have wept for him. 'If she believes she's in love with McGill, and I tackle her with it, she'll walk out on me and go to him. That he wouldn't want her as a permanent fixture in his life wouldn't occur to her—although seeing you two together might have raised a few doubts. If you want my opinion we've got to make him show his true colours before she commits herself to him completely. And that's where you come in. You must see that.'

She did, and she didn't like what she saw, but there was a limit to what sibling affection and loyalty could make her do.

'Then why not have it out with him? If all else fails, punch his arrogant nose!' she suggested through her teeth, trying not to acknowledge that if an argument between the two men degenerated to a brawl then McGill would walk away the winner.

'Don't think I wouldn't like to.' Jon laughed without humour. 'But Crane and I need his bank's funding. I've used Rowan, McGill and Cade before when I've had cash flow problems and they've funded several of Crane's projects. The negotiations on the south coast project are at a delicate stage. I can't afford to get on the wrong side of the bastard right now. We need to have completion of the project to coincide, as nearly as possible, with the opening of the Channel Tunnel, so time is tight—and that puts shopping around for another source of funding right out of the question.'

Jon wasn't a fool and he wasn't weak, but right now he sounded both. For as long as she could remember he had looked out for her, never once making her feel that the care of a much younger sister could be irksome, as it must, at times, have been.

On the death of their father he had stepped into his shoes, getting the already successful construction company ready for the twenty-first century. But now his guts and determination were being undermined by his wife's stupid infatuation with her boss. She blamed McGill far more than she blamed Marian. He was no more in love with his PA than he had been with all the others he had bedded. He took his pleasures where they offered—his reaction to her had been ample proof of that. She hated him, and all men like him.

'You'll do what you can?' Jon butted into her raging thoughts. 'If you can get him to agree to see you this weekend it will mean he'll drop Marian flat. She won't be able to ignore that, as she's obviously been trying to ignore the way he reacted to you last Saturday. And you can break the date when it comes down to it.'

Quilla closed her eyes defeatedly, her thick lashes lying heavily on her cheeks. She was trapped, and she knew it.

'I'll do what I can,' she promised grimly, wondering if Jon could have any idea of what she was letting herself in for. Breaking a date with Fraser McGill would be like waiting for an earthquake to happen.

But she could handle it, couldn't she?

For the sake of Jon's marriage, she had to!

CHAPTER THREE

HE MIGHT not turn up, of course.

Nevertheless, Quilla dressed with great care. Unlike the gold tissue dress she'd worn on Saturday, the black silk crêpe left everything to the imagination, skimming her willowy body, giving her a fragile look, a misleading impression which was emphasised by the way she had piled the glossy black weight of her hair on the top of her head in a vaguely Edwardian style, the slender gold earrings making her long white neck look as if it could be snapped between the fingers of one hand. If he came he wouldn't be able to accuse her of dressing to kill.

If he came...

Despite the promise her brother had extracted from her, she hoped Fraser McGill wouldn't come. Hoped with a desperation that made her feel ill. And her heart was drumming like a crazy thing as eight o'clock approached, and leapt into her throat to choke her as the doorbell rang.

Nico was out and wouldn't return until much later, so she grabbed her poppy-red silk shawl and jet-beaded bag and went to admit the brute, her heart now down in her high-heeled black silk shoes.

He was wearing elegantly tailored evening clothes, but the urbanity of his apparel only emphasised the toughness of his craggy features, the lean power of his aggressively masculine body.

'Come in,' she invited stiltedly, not because she wanted him under her roof but because she might just be able to convince him that she did have a prior engagement, was waiting for her escort, but would be free to see him over the weekend—for a date she would have no intention of keeping.

But it was a forlorn, pathetically over-optimistic hope, she recognised sickly as he answered, the huskiness in his voice sending shivers down her spine, 'Later, perhaps. I'd like that.' His meaning was horribly clear. 'But right now I have the car waiting.'

She would have a far better chance of persuading him to agree to see her over the coming weekend, and so cancel the arrangements he'd made with Marian, if she swallowed her pride and distaste and agreed to have dinner with him tonight. It wasn't a decision she was happy to make and she glanced across the street, wishing herself a million miles away.

A chauffeur-driven Rolls, no less, was waiting, she recognised dully. Defeatedly, she wrapped the scarlet shawl around her body because a chilly wind had sprung out of nowhere, and very quickly regretted it as she saw the sharp and unmistakable flicker of desire flare in those watchful grey eyes.

The shawl was a mistake, the red fringed silk making her look exotic, nullifying the effect of the understated black crêpe.

Feeling his eyes on her body, she stalked over to the Rolls, barely able to manage a smile for the uniformed chauffeur who sprang to open the rear door. She was, she admitted, more nervous than she had ever been in her life before, and scrambled with more haste than dignity as far as she could across the seat, the luxurious scent of leather making her stomach churn.

McGill got in beside her and the car moved off. He lounged back, his long legs stretched out at an angle, very relaxed, watching her.

'You did a remarkable disappearing act last weekend,' he commented, sounding more amused than annoyed, as if he could see the joke against himself, adding softly, 'Just as you'd grabbed my interest you disappeared in a puff of smoke. A tactical manoeuvre, I take it?'

If he was beginning to think that way then he was nearer the truth than he had any right to be, and her heart pumped alarmingly. He was far too astute, and she couldn't tell him the truth because that would ruin the object of the exercise so, for the time being, she would have to grit her teeth and allow the brute to believe she was aiming to join his string of lovers.

The very idea sickened her, made her feel unclean, but she managed to shake the feeling off and said crisply, 'Not at all. Pressure of business. That's something I'm sure you understand. Where are we going?'

She hoped she hadn't sounded as apprehensive as she felt—it was like being kidnapped—and he said smokily, 'To my house,' and that made her feel very much worse, because she would have felt relatively safe with him in a public restaurant. In his own home, just the two of them, she wouldn't feel safe at all.

The big car was whispering luxuriously through the quiet, elegant streets of Knightsbridge now, heading towards Belgravia, and Quilla shuddered.

'Cold?' McGill asked throatily, and she shook her head.

'A goose wandered over my grave.'

She was far from cold, too hot, if anything. She could feel drops of perspiration gathering in the palms of her hands and, looking sideways, she saw his knowing smile and wanted, quite desperately, to hit him. He was too damned sure of himself, arrogant male confidence oozing out of every pore, secure in the knowledge that she was just another female, intent on throwing herself at his head.

But she had nothing to be afraid of, she assured herself staunchly as the car slid to a halt outside an elegant Nash town house. The leaves of a plane tree rustled overhead as he escorted her over the wide pavement, and she wished she were a bird, up in the leafy branches, able to fly away.

But she wasn't and she couldn't, and she reminded herself again that she had absolutely nothing to fear.

Despite his reputation, he wasn't a brute. He was far too sophisticated to force her to do anything she didn't want to do. And she was fairly sophisticated herself, a successful woman in her own right, and surely she could hold him at arm's length until she'd got him to do what she and Jon wanted him to do, namely to demonstrate to the misguided Marian exactly what a perfidious louse he was!

Somewhat reassured, she was able to manage a smile for the stocky, middle-aged woman in grey who'd opened the door to them.

'Maggie Williams—she and her husband look after me. Williams just drove us,' McGill introduced, and Quilla surrendered her shawl, her golden eyes knowledgeably assessing the grace and space of the black and white tiled hall, the exquisitely carved balustrade of a staircase that soared to the second floor of the house, the magnificent crystal chandelier, and an antique console table that bore a single bowl of fragrant deep red roses.

He was a seriously wealthy man, she recognised as he ushered her through to a drawing-room, which was furnished in a tasteful mix of fine antiques, covetable paintings, discreetly luxurious fabrics.

But it wasn't his financial standing that made her feel as if her knees might give way. It was the sheer brain-numbing magnetism of the man. Even if he didn't have a penny to his name he would still have women swarming around him in droves.

And there was even more than that. He possessed a steely-eyed aura of power that made her mouth go dry, and when he placed a hand on the small of her back as he walked her over to an attractively upholstered sofa in front of the perfectly proportioned Adam fireplace the heat from the unexpected and unwanted contact sent fiery sensation racing all over her body.

Annoyed by the betraying tinge of colour she felt crawling over her pale skin, she concentrated on seating herself with some semblance of poise, willing her fluttering nerves to lie still. He had a dreadful effect on her, she thought worriedly as he walked over to the drinks cabinet. He made her feel small and feminine and utterly, utterly vulnerable. She had never reacted so strongly, or so much out of character, to any man ever before.

Guilty conscience, she informed herself tartly, crossing one silk-clad calf over the other. Simply knowing that her reason for being here at all was of dubious honesty, a rather devious charade, made her feel guilty as hell.

But he deserved it, didn't he? And, having met him, experienced his powerful charisma for herself, she could understand why some women might behave irrationally, lose their heads and their sense of balance when he was around.

Not that she would, of course. She knew what a heartless monster he was, and forewarned was certainly forearmed. But Marian, if her marriage had been going through a prolonged bad patch, as Jon had admitted it had, would have been easy prey for a man like Fraser McGill.

He thoroughly deserved a slap-down, she consoled her conscience, and felt equal almost to anything when he came to sit beside her, handing her a glass of sherry.

It was the brand she preferred, pale and dry, and she wondered if it was sheer coincidence or if he had remembered her tastes from the previous Saturday. Not that it signified, of course. She took a careful sip and searched for something to say to break a silence which was becoming painfully intimate.

'Have the Williamses been with you long?' It was, she had to admit to herself, an inane question, hardly sparkling conversation, but as she had the rest of the evening to get through, and, at the end of it, the unpleasant task of suggesting that they meet during the weekend, she felt that playing it safe for the moment was the most sensible thing to do.

Amusement warmed the dark grey eyes he turned in her direction, making her fingers tighten around the stem of her glass, reminding her horribly that the game she was playing was an enigma to her, the rules a closed book.

'I engaged them about four years ago when I bought this house. They're not old and devoted family retainers,' he told her drily, cynicism bracketing his mouth as he added, 'The McGill family, as such, is non-existent.'

'But you must have a family,' she objected, realising the stupidity of that remark when he drawled,

'I wasn't found under a gooseberry bush, no. But I might as well have been.' Which got her thinking, wondering if his apparent inability to form a lasting commitment to any one woman had its roots in his past. But she wasn't allowed to probe more deeply because he said, almost accusingly, 'Whereas you, of course, have strong, almost smothering family ties.'

'Hardly.' Her mouth straightened defensively. 'My mother was drowned when I was eight and my father was too busy mourning her to remember he had children.' Then, finding herself subjected to the full force of his cool analytical eyes, she wished the words unsaid. Displaying her past vulnerabilities to him was no part of her brief.

He said slowly, 'I know. But you have Jon. You and he have always been particularly close. He practically brought you up.'

And that comment shouldn't have surprised her. Jon was one of his clients and what Marian, as his PA, hadn't let slip, he would have made it his business to find out. A man like Fraser McGill would always have his clients thoroughly vetted. In his business he would have to take risks, but they would be painstakingly minimised where possible.

'But I'm sure we can find more interesting sub-
jects.' The edge had eased out of his voice; it was
rich dark honey now, and he had angled his lithe
body into the corner of the sofa, his eyes drifting
slowly over her body.

She felt as if he were stripping her naked, the
black dress no barrier at all to his accomplished
assessment, and any moment now he would say
something she wouldn't be able to negate with a
tart reply. Her skin crawled with an apprehension
that had nothing at all to do with the game she was
playing, and she could have wept with relief when
Maggie put her head round the door and cheerfully
announced that dinner was served.

As she shot to her feet with almost indecent haste,
Quilla wondered where the poise she'd always
prided herself on had gone. She felt as skittish as
a teenager, out of her depth, his hand on her arm
as he escorted her through to the small intimate
dining-room more possessive than it had any right
to be.

But, despite her nerve-quaking misgivings, dinner
turned out to be a totally relaxed affair. A creamy
mix of avocado and smoked salmon was followed
by thin slices of braised venison and meltingly
tender asparagus spears, accompanied by a fine
Chambertin which, Quilla suspected, contributed
almost as much to her strangely relaxed mood as
did Fraser's drily amusing conversation.

Coffee back in the drawing-room, with a fine
vintage cognac that further enhanced her sense of
well-being. If McGill had been anyone else she
would have said she couldn't remember having enjoyed an evening so much in years.

But then he touched her and everything changed. Just the lightest brush of his fingers as he took her empty coffee-cup, a small enough contact but capable of filling her body with sheet-fire sensation.

'Yes, I know,' he responded huskily to the small ragged gasp she couldn't disguise, his grey eyes narrowed and gleaming as they held hers. 'I know,' he repeated, acknowledging the reaction that had so shaken her, as if he had experienced it himself. And she watched with wide golden eyes as he put down the cup he had taken from her, her heart beating far too quickly because she knew he was going to kiss her.

And he did. It was completely inevitable. He drew her gently but inescapably into his arms and when his lips covered hers her whole world exploded into a million glittering shards of sensation, and she clung to him because her body was boneless, weak with a shattering need she had never experienced before. He was the rock she had to cling to in the strange wild sea of desire that engulfed her, threatening to submerge her completely.

The tiny metallic sound of the zip at the back of her dress brought her partially back to her senses and her mind struggled to surface from the overwhelming maelstrom of physical need, fighting to restore order in a world gone suddenly out of control.

But an involuntary shudder shook her as his lips left hers and began to move with exquisite sorcery over the contours of her face, tasting the pale, delicate skin, learning, with a dedicated thoroughness that left her breathless, the structure of the bones beneath, his hands pushing aside the fine fabric of her dress, caressing the naked skin of her back.

In a moment, she knew, she would be lost, too weakened to withstand the sensory bombardment he was so expertly subjecting her to, and she bit down hard on her lower lip, tasting her own blood on the passion-bruised flesh, the self-inflicted pain going some way to negate the crazed clamour of her senses.

True to form, the wretch believed she was a pushover, she reminded herself bitterly. And the game had progressed one stage further and she could almost hear Jon's applause.

She felt sickened, not only by his behaviour, but by hers. But to slap Fraser's arrogant face and stalk out of here—which would give her the greatest satisfaction in the world—would mean she had sacrificed her principles for nothing. Everything hinged on the coming weekend.

And her blood ran cold as he muttered thickly, 'God, I want you! I've been in a fever since I first set eyes on you.'

His arms tightened around her and the hardness of him left her in no doubt that what he said was true. And Fraser McGill was a man who made sure he got what he wanted, and if she lost control again, even for a second, she would be powerless to fight her own body's treacherous responses.

Grabbing at the fragile remnants of her poise, she extricated herself from his encircling arms, her voice unsteady as she fought to temper a very definite rejection with a tenuous promise.

'Please—don't rush me, Fraser. It's too soon.'

Something flared darkly in the depths of his smoky eyes and, unbelievably, she, too, felt the sharp pain of unfulfilment and cursed the chemistry that made her so stingingly aware of him. But, whatever the nature of the emotion that had momentarily struggled for supremacy in the smouldering depths of his eyes, he successfully conquered it, his smile wry as he admitted, 'You are quite right, of course,' and went to press a bell which was discreetly hidden in the hearth recess, his urbanity now a cloak that hid his thoughts in suave anonymity. 'Williams will drive you home.'

His smile was fleeting, very smooth, and it told her nothing at all, and Quilla reached shaking fingers to deal with her zip, to tidy the wandering tendrils of her hair. She said, 'Thank you,' and felt curiously empty because, after her rejection, he was clearly dismissing her.

It was a reaction she might have expected, and to allow herself to feel strangely hurt because of it was nothing less than gross stupidity. She no longer interested him because, quite obviously, all he'd had in mind for her was a one-night stand. In his mind, any further attempts to get her into his bed would be a waste of his valuable time. She wasn't worth the effort. And instead of making her feel unclean, or angry, the knowledge made her feel lonely, lost. Which was crazy, unworthy of her.

As the chauffeur appeared McGill instructed coolly, 'The car, please, Williams. And Miss Kent's wrap.'

And because the silence that followed when Williams withdrew was too intense to be borne, Quilla said tightly, lying through her teeth, 'It's been a delightful evening. Thank you.'

'The first of many.' His answer came as a total surprise. She'd been so sure he wouldn't want to see her again, that her virginal protestations had put him off her for life. And the glint of amusement deep in his clever grey eyes did something unwelcome to her equilibrium, made her feel as transparent as a five-year-old.

He obviously hadn't given up on her and, strangely, all things considered, it put her on a high, and she found herself saying recklessly, her lips curving with an enticement she was unaware of, 'This weekend, perhaps?' and held her breath because if he agreed to see her he wouldn't be keeping his date with Marian, and she would have done what Jon had begged her to do.

Williams was in the doorway again, the scarlet shawl in his hands, and McGill took it from him and turned back to her, wrapping the silk around her body with a deliberation that was weakeningly erotic, lowering his head to touch her parted lips with his, the smile in his husky voice sending shivers down her spine as he said softly, 'Alas, no. I'm tied up for the entire weekend, but I'll be in touch, I promise.'

Her eyes widening, she stared at him. She knew she must look like a pole-axed fool but was incapable of doing anything about it. Her whole body had gone numb, very cold, but she knew that burning anger would come later, and shame.

She had played the game and lost. Fraser McGill meant to have his cake and eat it. He wasn't prepared to cancel his weekend with the adoring Marian. Men like him fed on women's blind adoration. And when that pleasurable interlude was over he would crook his finger and expect her to come running.

She wouldn't, of course. And after tonight she would run a mile if he came anywhere near her. She wouldn't be seeing him, not again, and she felt cold, and in pain, but that was the anger waiting to break out, she assured herself, as, with an arm lying across her shoulders, he escorted her out to the waiting Rolls, Williams already behind the wheel.

And she couldn't summon the wit to make a snappy retort when, catching her briefly to the hard, impeccable length of his body, he murmured throatily, 'Williams will see you safely home. If I drove you myself I wouldn't be able to trust myself not to cross your demarcation line.'

CHAPTER FOUR

'WHY don't you come with me?' Nico was ready to leave, very flamboyant in a black Cordovan, a collarless black shirt and skin-tight white trousers. And Quilla, moodily sipping her third black coffee of the morning, shook her head.

He was due to meet a photographer and journalist from one of the prestigious glossies at the warehouse. She'd set up the interview weeks ago, an indepth insight into the way one of the country's top young designers worked, and that was it, as far as she was concerned. She was the one who set the wheels in motion, kept them oiled, applied the brakes occasionally and, this morning in particular, she didn't feel like being around to hold Nico's hand.

'Well, you should do something to cheer yourself up. You look as if you're expecting the end of the world.'

She tried to smile and found she couldn't. It was going to be another hot day and much as she normally loved the hustle and noise and excitement of the capital she had the feeling that this weekend was going to turn out to be utterly depressing.

She longed, suddenly, to be somewhere cool and green and quiet, but when Nico suggested tartly, 'Go and spend the weekend at Marshbrook—fresh air's good for wet blankets,' all she could do was shake her head and reply with a briskness that went against the grain,

'If you don't get going you'll be late for your appointment, and I've got plenty of work to occupy me, so thanks for your concern, but it's entirely misplaced.'

The thought of going to Marshbrook depressed her even more than the idea of sweltering in London. Jon had phoned her early on this morning, his voice bitter.

'When I got home last night she'd already left, just a note to say she'd be back on Monday, and a phone number. I called at nine this morning, some female answered, sounded halfway round the bend, said she'd never heard of Marian Kent. Hell, Quilla, I don't what's going on—at least,' she heard the iron in his voice, 'I do, and it's pulling me to pieces.'

Confessing that she hadn't been able to persuade McGill to date her over the weekend, thus keeping him away from Marian and the illicit few days they had obviously planned, had made her feel more than inadequate. It was not a sensation she enjoyed, and it was unjustified because, although she had reluctantly done what she could, she had found the scheme distasteful, right from the start, so her voice emerged more sharply than she had meant it to as she stated, 'It was an unrealistic idea from the beginning and it didn't work. You were off your head if you thought it would. Anyway, what are you going to do now?'

If he suggested she had anything more to do with Fraser McGill she would categorically refuse. But he said heavily, 'Bring the whole sordid mess out into the open. There's nothing else I can do now, is there? As you know, I'd hoped to avoid that kind of confrontation, hoped we'd be able to show her exactly what he is. But it's gone way beyond that now.'

Jon rarely lost his temper, but the cold rage in his voice had been unmistakable. He had a cool, logical brain, able to see both sides of any given situation. She knew he was blaming himself for the erosion of his marriage, had been willing to forgive and forget that Marian had temporarily believed herself to be in love with her boss. He had been willing to try to work things out, and, once Marian had seen through McGill, to start again. But by spending the weekend with him, becoming his lover, Marian had dug her own grave as far as Jon was concerned.

Quilla had put the phone down thoughtfully. She wouldn't like to be in her sister-in-law's shoes when she returned on Monday. She didn't blame Jon. If she ever married and discovered her partner had been unfaithful she would be devastated.

Despite the open window her office was hot and airless, the rumble of traffic in the street below an intrusion she could have done without. And, despite her tart observations to Nico, she had nothing to do that couldn't wait.

Idly, she began to twist her heavy hair up off the nape of her neck and into a knot on the top of her head, but dropped it as the doorbell pealed. She wasn't expecting anyone and, ashamed of her disloyalty, hoped it wasn't Jon, bent on pouring out all his marital troubles yet again.

Suddenly reluctant, she opened the door and felt her stupid heart leap inside her.

'You!' She couldn't help the smile that lit up her whole face, made her golden eyes gleam.

'Yes,' he acknowledged, his firm mouth bracketed in a slow smile, the grey eyes warm. He was wearing casual denim jeans and a matching jacket over a well-washed black T-shirt and he shouldered his way past her, his thumbs hooked into the scuffed leather belt that spanned his lean waist.

Fraser McGill was the last person she had expected to see. She had never wanted to set eyes on him again, she reminded herself uselessly, and wondered why the vague feeling of depression had vanished, leaving her feeling giddy.

'You said you were tied up all weekend.' Unknown to herself, she made the statement sound like an accusation, her poise deserting her utterly as the dark grey eyes swept her body in open appreciation.

She was wearing a full, fine cotton skirt, a toning tawny sleeveless top, but beneath the slow caress of his eyes she felt naked.

'I untied myself,' he told her quietly, the thick black bar of his brows rising as he noted her stupefied expression. 'I found I couldn't keep away. Is that so surprising? The car's outside and Maggie's packed a hamper. It's too nice a day to stay cooped up in the city.' He held out a well-made, capable hand. 'Coming?'

Where to? she wanted to ask, but didn't. The total unexpectedness of his arrival had addled her brain. She couldn't seem to think straight. And then the full import of what had happened struck her and she went weak with relief.

He had, after all, cancelled his weekend with Marian, in order to see her. But it was early days, only Saturday morning, and if she told him to get lost, which was what she had vowed to do if he ever asked her to spend time with him again, he would undoubtedly go straight to the waiting Marian, making some excuse to cover his delay. He would be good at making excuses.

But something inside her warned her against taking that outstretched hand, so she said briskly, 'What had you in mind? I'd planned to spend the day working.'

'Then do as I did. Alter your plans.' The curious directness of his stare was disconcerting and, for a moment, she felt profoundly uneasy, threatened. But loyalty to her brother overcame her misgivings. To tell him she wanted nothing more to do with him would send him straight to her sister-in-law so she answered nervily,

'Just give me a few minutes,' and saw his eyes narrow, as if she puzzled him, before he replied tonelessly,

'No more than one. You don't need to change; we'll be spending the day in the sticks.' Then he walked through the open door to her office with the frightening self-assurance that was so much a part of his character in blatant evidence, leaving her tongue-tied, her own self-confidence at an all-time low.

She was actually trembling with nervous reaction when she gained the sanctuary of her bedroom. No man had ever had this effect on her before.

But it wasn't McGill, personally, who made her feel so uncharacteristically jumpy, she reasoned punchily. It was the game she was playing. Her character was straightforward and direct—she wasn't used to behaving deviously. But Jon had successfully used emotional blackmail and she was too fond of him to back out now.

With unsteady hands she applied a little make-up, a burnt umber eyeshadow and a gloss of copper lipstick. She wasn't going to bother to change, it would take too long, and Fraser McGill was the type to march upstairs and fetch her if he thought she was keeping him waiting.

But she did take time to pile her hair on the top of her head. The day was far too hot and sticky to leave it hanging around her shoulders. A dab of cologne on her pulse-points and she was ready to go. And meeting her huge haunted eyes in the mirror reminded her of how little she was looking forward to the day ahead.

No wonder Fraser had looked so puzzled when her reluctance to spend the day with him had been so obvious. She had deliberately sought to capture his interest at that dinner party, had invited him to date her this weekend, and yet when he'd actually shown up on her doorstep she'd behaved like a jittery cat. He probably thought she was half round the twist!

When she arrived downstairs he was still in her office, engrossed by her wall-chart schedules, and he turned as she hovered in the open doorway, as if he'd sensed her presence. He certainly couldn't have heard her; her approach had been silent.

'You're quite a high flyer, I've heard,' he remarked, his keen eyes holding hers, and she wondered who he'd been discussing her with but wouldn't give him the satisfaction of asking. She hated the idea of him checking up on her; it made her feel defenceless.

Covering an involuntary shudder, she replied scornfully, 'I enjoy my work and I'm good at it, and I earn enough to have jam on my bread occasionally. And if that makes me a high flyer——' She shrugged dismissively. 'Shall we go?'

Far from giving him a successful 'back-off' signal, she seemed to have amused him, she decided wrathfully as he placed a hand on the small of her back and walked her to the door. The devil had merely given her a huge, delighted grin, seeming to strip away all her snippy defences. She had the horrible feeling that she could hide very little from him.

But, determined not to fudge the opportunity that had been handed her on a plate—the chance to keep McGill away from her foolish sister-in-law—Quilla forced herself to relax as he manoeuvred the car through the city traffic with an aggressive panache that would have had her on the edge of her seat, biting her nails, if her mind hadn't been preoccupied with the need to appear at ease in his company, at least for the time being.

The Rolls wasn't in evidence today; he was driving a racy Lotus Elan and he hadn't said where they were headed but they were travelling through Surrey and once they were beyond the stockbroker belt Fraser seemed to shed his suave urbanity, to become another person.

There was a tension about him she hadn't seen before, he seemed deep in the coils of a blinding nervous energy that was only tenuously under leash.

He was driving more slowly now, of course, because the narrow leafy lanes were winding, as if uncertain and uncaring of their destination, typical of ancient English highways. But Fraser knew where he was going, he wouldn't be Fraser McGill if he didn't, and there was a strangely electrifying glow deep in his eyes, making them look more silver than grey as he glanced at her briefly, imparting, 'I'm taking you to Old Ford. I want your reactions.'

That strange inner excitement of his must be contagious, Quilla decided as a *frisson* of nameless sensation left her feeling breathless, but she managed a small cool smile.

'Where and what is Old Ford?' and turned her head, looking out of the window at the high leafy verges because, for some unknown reason, looking at him made her feel dangerously alive, more mindlessly exhilarated than she had ever felt before.

'Just a cottage,' he told her, his voice dark and warm. 'I acquired it a few weeks ago. It will be the first real home I've ever had.'

In any other man she would have tied that statement in with his air of barely suppressed excitement. But not this man. He was wealthy in his own right and, from what she'd been able to gather, came from a privileged background. Besides, he already had a prestigious home in Belgravia. She'd been there, seen it.

And he wasn't the type to get enthusiastic over a country cottage—a less tamed and domesticated, pipe and slippers man she had yet to meet. She opened her mouth to take him up on that but he stalled her.

'There's been a bridge over what used to be a ford for the last hundred-odd years, but that's where the cottage got its name from. You'll see it in a second or two.' He swung the car on to a narrow track between hedgerows dripping with honeysuckle and wild roses.

The brook beneath the stone bridge was only a trickle now, but Quilla guessed it would become a torrent in the winter rains, and the cottage itself was like something out of a fairy-tale—low thatched roofs, a sturdy timber frame and a lushly overgrown garden that hadn't seen a spade or pruning shears in a decade.

'It's adorable!' she exclaimed involuntarily, her long golden eyes gleaming with enthusiastic appreciation. Bathed in the warmth of the early June sun, the soft air heavy with the scent of blossoms, the only sounds those of bumble bees, wood pigeons and the lazy murmurings of the brook, it was indeed idyllic. But she couldn't see a man as dynamic as Fraser settling for long in such quiet, rustic surroundings.

However, her spontaneous reaction seemed, for some reason or other, to have pleased him, and the smile he gave her as he opened the door at her side to help her out of the car made her toes curl. And he actually seemed ten years younger as he showed her over the house, pointing out the obvious when he said how much needed to be done before the place was habitable.

'And you really intend living here?' she asked as they eventually emerged from a side door into a miniature jungle of untended soft fruit bushes.

The sun was hot on her bare arms and suddenly she was stingingly aware of the man who stood so close to her. The awareness, she recognised, had been growing from the first moment of seeing him at that dinner party. And right now she felt far too keyed-up to trust herself to behave in her normal poised manner. Her ability to cope with most situations, most people, seemed to have deserted her.

If he touched her she would burst into flame because all her stupid mind could think of was the way she had felt when he'd held her that night in Belgravia, kissed her, shaped her body lovingly with his hands, tasted her...

But he didn't touch her, he merely stepped out on to a little paved path that was almost completely overgrown with tiny wild pansies, their purple and yellow faces exquisitely innocent, and told her,

'Weekends only, to begin with. But later I hope to be here more permanently.'

'But you have a home in London.' She felt some comment was expected of her, although watching his lean, dangerously masculine body as he strode down the path in front of her was having a totally unnerving effect on her. She was amazed that her voice had come out at all, considering the size of the odd constriction in her throat.

He had left his denim jacket in the car and the sleeveless black T-shirt moulded the lithe musculature of his shoulders and back to aching perfection, the rangy width of his shoulders making his waist and hips look even narrower by contrast.

There was no doubt about it, he was a spectacularly attractive devil and, for the first time, she felt a sneaking sympathy for Marian.

'A house, not a home,' he corrected, holding the disintegrating wicket at the end of the path for her to pass through.

She said intuitively, suddenly in tune with him, 'Necessary window-dressing for the big City banker.'

He turned the bone-bending power of his slow appreciative smile on her, his eyes warm. 'Got it in one. Bright girl!'

His arm around her shoulders, the slight pressure of his fingers on the bare flesh of her upper arm, was something she could have done without. It scrambled her brain, sent weakening sensations through her entire body, and she had to force herself to concentrate on what he was saying.

'Until I bought Old Ford I hadn't had a place I felt I could call home. There were houses I lived in, of course, but never a place I could relate to personally.'

'Not even when you were a child?' Something beyond her control drew the question from her. She hadn't meant to probe; she didn't want to know anything about him because getting to know him on a deeper level would bring them closer. She didn't want that. She knew intuitively that it would represent a danger she was no longer sure she could handle.

But somehow the words had been wrenched from her and his deep velvety voice made her shiver inside as he told her, 'Particularly not then. I was born in Hong Kong where my father was in banking. He had to be the archetypal Old Colonial—lived for his work, assured of, and proud of, his status. He created a financial empire and, as far as he was concerned, I was his stake in the future, the obligatory son to inherit all he had achieved. When he died five years ago my deepest regret was that I had never really known him.'

Something, certainly not in the level tone of voice he used, or his pragmatic choice of words, touched the deep well of compassion inside her.

She stood aside, purposely distancing herself, watching with guarded eyes as he removed a small wicker hamper and cool-box from the car. She didn't welcome the sudden feeling of empathy, she didn't want to admit that he could deserve her compassion. It would be infinitely preferable to continue to believe him to be undeserving of anyone's sympathy, to see him as a bastard who was as determinedly ruthless in his sex-life as he was in his business dealings.

There was a grassy clearing beside the brook where it bordered his property and he left her there, the dim green light filtering through the trees giving a mysterious dimension to his aggressively masculine looks, adding a subtler level of danger.

Quilla shivered, and he noticed, of course he did, and he asked, sounding concerned, 'Cold? We can find somewhere to eat in the sun, if you'd prefer.'

It was cool beneath the trees but after the heat of the sun the shade was welcome, the clear liquid note of running water, the rustle of leaves and sleepy birdsong something she needed, a salve for nerves foolishly overstretched.

'It's fine here.' She made her voice matter-of-fact and sank down gracefully on the short fine grass, the tawny cotton of her skirt falling around the elegant length of her legs like the petals of a flower.

They talked lightly as he laid out the food, poured chilled white wine into the cut crystal flutes that Maggie had carefully packed in layers of tissue paper. It was like being transported back in time, she thought idly, breaking into the light crust of a delicious game pasty with a silver Georgian fork. Rather Edwardian, very gracious. No plastic plates and beakers but fine china, silver and crystal. And then she spoiled the dreamy, out-of-time atmosphere, made everything too personal and immediate when she asked, 'And what about your mother?' And could have bitten her tongue out, because didn't she know how unwise it was to get to know him better?

If she knew what made him tick, the circumstances that had made him the man he was, then there was the danger that she might begin to empathise with him and that, coupled with his disastrous male charisma, could be very dangerous indeed.

'Mother?' There was nothing dismissive at all about the arching movement of one strongly defined brow, merely slightly amused tolerance. 'She was, and is, a social butterfly, even less interested in the parental role than my father—if that were possible.'

He had finished eating and was lying on the grass, stretched out beside her, his dark head propped on one hand. 'We lived in a beautiful house just above the golf course, one of the few open spaces in that crowded colony. Five indoor servants and three full-time gardeners. She never had to do a thing but spend the money Father made, and look glamorous. She did both superlatively well. I was very young when I was went to be educated in England, and saw my parents very rarely. When I did see them I got the impression that they scarcely knew who I was. And don't think I'm whingeing...' He smiled into her eyes, making her heart thump. 'In fact I'm grateful for the manner of my upbringing. It taught me to be self-sufficient, to avoid the trap of becoming emotionally dependent on anyone else, needing the comfortable placebo of love—and all that entails. But perhaps you can't understand that?'

He ran the fingers of one hand lightly over the cool skin of her arm, setting it on fire. Her mouth went dry. Throughout the day, and despite herself, their relationship had been growing, deepening, and there was an unsafe intimacy now in the way he was looking at her, in the indolent sureness of his touch.

'You're a ravishingly lovely woman, Quilla,' he went on softly, his grey eyes taking on the hypnotic quality of deep dark water. 'From what I've learned you're also highly intelligent, an achiever. And in its own way your childhood must have been almost as lonely as mine—yet you still haven't learned the wisdom of self-sufficiency. You cling too tightly to Jon.'

He leant over to put his mouth against hers and the warmth of his lips shocked her, held her immobile, stunned by the sensations that sent fever racing through her blood. 'It's time to let him go. He has life of his own now, apart from you. He has a wife.'

It was his mention of Marian that did it, brought her back to wisdom, to the sickening recognition of who and what he was.

He was talking about the need for emotional independence, pointing out, quite rightly, that she and Jon were perhaps too close—neglecting, of course, to mention that he was encouraging Jon's wife in her futile infatuation, had intended to become her lover this weekend. He was a vile hypocrite, preaching one thing and doing the other!

'What would you know about family ties, affection?' she sniped. 'You wouldn't recognise a real relationship if it hit you in the eye! You've already admitted you don't believe in love.'

She got tightly to her feet, anger eating into her. He knew nothing—nothing of how Jon's generous brotherly affection, support and understanding had held her together when she'd been too young and hurt to battle on her own.

And what did McGill care, anyway? How could he care when, as far as he was concerned, Jon's wife—the woman he had been at such pains to mention—was his for the taking, fair game, easily fooled by his superficial charm and just as easily dropped when a more entertaining prospect, in the shape of herself, proposed itself!

She didn't know why there were tears in her eyes when he intercepted her headlong flight, but there were. Stinging emotional tears that turned her eyes to topaz.

'Calm down.' Strong hands held her, twisted her round to face him. 'You've got me wrong. I believe in love—how could I not? I might as well say I didn't ''believe in'' double-decker buses. It happens—but not for me. In any case,' his mouth twisted wryly, 'we're discussing your emotional needs, not mine. There comes a time when we all have to let go,' he stated gently, misinterpreting her obvious distress.

She knew that circumstances had made herself and her brother closer than most siblings and that Jon could be insensitive when he rammed home the fact that Marshbrook belonged as much to his sister as it did to himself and his wife. And she had often remonstrated with him when his interest in her life had become too possessive, telling him that she was all grown-up now, more than capable of standing on her own two feet. No, letting go of her brother didn't distress her, what did upset her was McGill's treachery.

Yet it shouldn't, she knew it shouldn't. He meant less than nothing to her. She had known precisely the type of man he was when she had embarked on the distasteful exercise of trying to keep him away from Marian this weekend.

'But letting go doesn't mean losing out.' His inescapable hands slid round to her shoulder-blades, disturbing yet strangely comforting, too. 'There are other relationships that can be far more rewarding, infinitely more exciting.'

His voice had lowered huskily, his meaning unmistakable as his hands exerted a gentle pressure, moving her closer so that their bodies touched from breast to thigh, and the cool green air of the woodland glade suddenly became heated, enervating her, yet making her pulses race.

His hands were describing circles on her back now, shaping her slender wrist, sliding downwards with erotic expertise to mould the feminine flare of her hips, drawing her suddenly compliant body even closer to his.

Her heart was racing, her body sheer sensation, made weak and will-less by the awesome proximity of his. She had neither the strength nor the wit to pull away and his mouth was tasting her skin, sliding erotically over her face, down the arching length of her throat and on to the skin that covered her fragile collarbones.

And then, as if he knew she had neither the strength or desire to move away, his hands came up to cup her face. Gently, so gently, the liquid grey eyes holding the molten gold of hers, holding her very soul, stamping his power and mastery on a will already weakened by the vital and undeniable force of sexual chemistry. And he said slowly, as if tasting each word, 'I've wanted you since the moment I first saw you. You're a drug in my veins, a flame in my soul. You burn me with need.' And then his mouth claimed hers, the exquisitely slow master strokes of his tongue making a statement of intent, a wordless declaration of a future more total possession.

Quilla shuddered, her arms clinging now, shaken beyond sense or reason. She had always been too engrossed in her career to think of anything as time-consuming as falling in love.

In love? Was she losing her mind? No way, no way on this sweet earth!

Her groan of protest was smothered at source beneath the renewed sensual exploration of his lips as she inwardly struggled to repudiate her brief moment of insanity. She had to be certifiable if she thought, for one moment, that what was happening to her had anything whatsoever to do with love.

Her knees were so weak that to curve her body into the support of his was natural, so natural that her bemused mind hardly registered the way he lowered her to the ground, and her mouth was trembling with passion, trembling far too much to form a protest when he slid his hand beneath the hem of her top and curved it round one hardened, sensitised breast and then the other.

His touch was exquisitely gentle, yet infinitely possessive, tormenting her, and her whole body began to quiver with a need that was almost unbearable, making her ache. Someone groaned thickly, she wasn't sure if the sound came from her throat or from his, but she could feel the heavy race of his heartbeats beneath the palms of her hands.

'God, how I need you!' he muttered raggedly, his mouth against the silky skin of her throat, his body, half covering hers, already fully aroused, overpoweringly masculine, his hands making an erotic exploration of her body, creating havoc. 'It was instinctive and elemental from the moment I saw you. And it was the same for you. I saw it in your eyes.' His lips were teasing the corner of her mouth now, making utterly sensational forays into her inner sweetness, and one hand was caressing her thighs, finding the soft, willing, melting flesh.

An explosion of primitive need reduced her quivering body to supine, utterly feminine receptiveness, but her mind struggled fuzzily with his words. Had it been the same for her? A journey into the vibrant, shattering world of elemental desire? A journey he had embarked on with his eyes wide open, with no thought in his head of love because, self-admittedly, lust was the only emotion he could take on board, she half blinded by her total ignorance of how it could be. If she allowed it to be.

And she wouldn't. She couldn't.

Not if she was to keep her self-respect. Sexual satisfaction, just for the sake of it, was not her style. Already, deep inside her, an insistent throbbing had begun and she knew enough to realise that in a second or two she would be beyond help, out of control and uncaring of the consequences.

She had known all along that she was susceptible to this man, known it at some deep level of her consciousness right from the start. She had run from the danger then and must run from it now.

And she knew she could extricate herself with no trouble at all.

Marian would be kicking her heels in some out-of-the-way hotel, perhaps even returned home by now because her would-be lover hadn't shown up. So it was perfectly safe to show her hand. End the game.

'Hold on there.' Amazingly, her voice emerged quite coolly, although that achievement had been one of the most difficult things she had ever had to do. And her tone was crisp as she stabbed out, 'The only interest I ever had in you was the desire to keep you away from my sister-in-law.'

She felt him go very still. He didn't say anything, not for long moments, and then he demanded, 'Say that again.'

She did, pulling her still shaky body into a sitting position, her arms clasped round her knees, her long black hair now free of restricting pins, falling around her face, hiding her expression, the stupid, unaccountable shadow of pain in her eyes.

'I know you've been seeing Marian on a fairly regular basis—and I don't mean at work,' she said, her voice stilted now, her lips stiff with the effort it took to control the stupid trembling. 'Supposedly, you and she were working late. I discovered you weren't.' She kept Jon's name out of it deliberately. Much as her brother disliked McGill personally—and he had every reason to—he still needed the bank's backing.

She was staring straight ahead, her long golden eyes on the trees that overhung the opposite bank of the brook, not seeing them, but her voice was controlled, as cool and calm as the softly shadowed woodland air as she told him, 'When I learned she was planning to spend this weekend away with a friend no one had ever heard her so much as mention before, I got worried. And when I saw her coming out of your room at Marshbrook—you were as good as naked, by the way—and I saw you touch her face, like a lover, I knew I had to do something to try and save my brother's marriage.' Unconsciously, her voice had hardened, taking an edge of steel on board, and she added, 'I'd heard that you find it impossible to resist an open invitation from a presentable female. In fact, your bed-hopping proclivities are legendary. So I decided to set out to get your interest, to get you to drop Marian this weekend. Which you did. It will show her what a louse you really are, make her see that Jon is worth a dozen of you.'

He hadn't said a word, he'd let her spill it all out, explain the degrading game she'd been playing. But his very silence had a tangible quality. It surrounded her, isolated her, chilled her to the bone.

Almost panicking now because she knew his anger at the way she had used him would be monumental, she stood up, began putting her clothes in order, her fingers shaking, ending defiantly, with a recklessness she couldn't control, even though it privately astounded her, 'So you see, the interest has only been on your side. You leave me quite cold.'

He was still on the ground, his head propped on one hand, the grey eyes mocking, the sensual mouth curved as if he had a secret, not for sharing, and he drawled, his tone wicked, 'Forgive me if I find myself unable to believe in your lack of interest. But, in any case, you've talked yourself into a pretty tight corner, my pet.'

Suddenly, he was on his feet, standing over her, making her heart pump with alarm. His mouth was curved with what could have been derision and she felt totally threatened, unbelievably alone and vulnerable, and something clamped an icy hand around her heart as he informed her smoothly, 'As you pointed out, my interest has been aroused. And you should learn never to tweak the tail of a sleeping tiger unless you're fully prepared to take the consequences.'

Again, inescapable hands cupped her face, forcing her to meet that cool mocking gaze.

'I fully intend to see a great deal of you in the future, to make you burn for me as I burn for you. That is the consequence you were too arrogant to see and, to put it crudely, my pet, I intend to bed you, possess you, own you in every sense of the word.'

As a threat it was devastating. For a long moment she was too stunned to speak and then she blurted, 'And if I refuse to have anything more to do with you?'

The words came out in a scalding rush, bursting past the terrible constriction in her throat, her heart racing as if it would burst free of her body. The mind-pictures he had conjured just now had flooded her with a shameful, wanton response, but he couldn't force her to have anything more to do with him. Of course he couldn't!

But he could.

'Refuse away, it's entirely up to you. But if you do,' he added very softly, his eyes wicked, 'I'll go straight back to Marian. And don't think I wouldn't.'

CHAPTER FIVE

QUILLA was already at Marshbrook before Jon had left for work on Monday morning. She found him gloomily chewing on toast in the kitchen.

'Is Marian back?' She sounded edgy, and she was.

Jon said, 'No. Help yourself to coffee if you want some.'

He looked older, harder, his face grey, and as she poured coffee from the scarlet enamel pot he asked, as if not terribly interested, 'What brings you here at this hour?'

She perched on a corner of the kitchen table, cradling her mug in her hands, unsure of what to say, what to leave out. She could tell him that he'd been right all along, that McGill had even admitted to having an affair with his PA but, on the whole, she didn't think that would be very helpful. Choosing her words carefully, she told him, 'Wherever Marian was on Saturday, she wasn't with Fraser McGill. I was,' and waited to see what his reaction would be.

'And on Sunday? She didn't come home and, before you ask, I didn't try the number she left again. I don't like making myself look an idiot.' He wasn't impressed by her news. It was as if all emotion had drained out of him over this weekend.

'I don't know about McGill, but I worked,' she admitted. And she had. Furiously. All the time waiting to see if McGill would carry out his threat to contact her again, demand her company... Or else!

But he hadn't called by, or phoned her, and when she'd finished up and gone to bed at just after midnight she hadn't known whether she felt disappointed or not.

'Well, that's it, isn't it?' Jon stated flatly. He got up from the table, leaving his barely touched breakfast. 'She's due back here at around eleven. At least, that's what she said in her note. She may never come back, for all I know.' Or care, his tone implied, and Quilla's heart ached for him. He picked up his briefcase. 'Lock the door behind you when you leave.'

So her sister-in-law was coming here, not going straight back to work. It was what Quilla was banking on. It was well past time, to her mind, for a little straight talking.

In the past, Marian's obvious resentment had prevented them getting close, but it was time someone told her that her stupid infatuation for her boss was ruining her marriage—if it hadn't already gone beyond the point of no return.

Telling her that Fraser would have no hesitation in dropping her flat provided she, Quilla, agreed to continue seeing him, with all that entailed, should shock her into some kind of sense. And if she asked Jon's forgiveness he might be willing to forget the whole sordid business. He was still in love with her.

McGill hadn't denied their hole-and-corner affair, and why should he? His gentlemanly instincts were around nil as far as Quilla could see. He was a sexual opportunist, heedlessly taking his pleasures, uncaring of who got hurt. He was tough, unsentimental, and his early life had made living without love seem normal. Emotional ties were not for him, he had told her that much. If he didn't need love, then why should others?

And her reasons for wanting to put Marian in the picture weren't entirely altruistic, she admitted as she washed and put away Jon's breakfast things, thankful that Mrs Hodge always had every Monday off.

True, it would open Marian's eyes to reality, but it would also remove McGill's leverage. Seeing him again, as he had insisted on as his price for ending his involvement with his PA, would be the most dangerous thing she had ever done.

Because he'd been right when he'd stated that the attraction between them had been instantaneous and cataclysmic, and that afternoon beside the brook had shown her how powerfully responsive she was to his lovemaking. She had no immunity where he was concerned.

And all she meant to him was the challenge of a new sexual conquest, and her reckless and false statement about her total lack of interest in him, in any capacity, had probably made him all the more determined to prove her wrong, to have her in his bed. Women found him irresistible, and he would never back gracefully away no matter how often and loudly she insisted that she, for one, did not.

She didn't fool herself into believing that she could ever mean anything special to him. Women would never be more than a sideshow to him; his work was the love of his life.

When she gave herself to a man it would be because she loved and respected him, planned to spend the rest of her life with him, bear his children, be a part of him.

So breaking McGill's leverage was top priority.

It was over two hours later before she heard the distinctive engine sound of the VW Beetle Marian drove, and Quilla, her nerves in shreds, leapt to hold the front door open, her accusatory, 'Where the hell have you been?' wiping the dreamy smile from the other woman's face.

Before her hasty and not at all welcoming remark, Marian had looked more relaxed and cheerful then she had seen her in ages. And that, Quilla thought sourly, was because that louse McGill had probably not long left her. He didn't miss a trick.

But she felt marginally better when Marian said worriedly, anxiety puckering her forehead, 'What's wrong? It's not Jon, is it?'

'Jon's fine,' Quilla assured her quickly. There was some hope for the marriage, after all. Marian wasn't so far gone in her infatuation for that devil McGill that she had ceased to care about her husband.

At the mere thought of Fraser McGill Quilla shuddered, the *frisson* of sensation that rushed through her not entirely unpleasant. The loathsome man affected her as no other man had ever done before, and the knowledge filled her with self-revulsion. 'There's nothing wrong with Jon,' she repeated. 'At least, not physically.'

The colour that had returned to Marian's face fled again and she moistened her lips before asking thickly, 'What's that supposed to mean?'

'We'd better go inside. I'll make some coffee— I think we're both going to need it.' She didn't relish hauling the other woman over the coals, or having to explain her own part in the sordid charade. Chewing on her wide lower lip, she decided to leap in with both feet. To tread gently might have the effect of glamorising the situation, making Marian view her sordid affair with McGill in a more romantic light than it deserved. Better that she should see the monster in his true colours immediately.

So she put the two mugs of coffee down on the table and stated baldly, 'In case you're wondering where Fraser McGill really was on Saturday, he was with me, telling me that he would end his affair with you on the condition that I agree to see him.'

Watching the look of complete bewilderment chase away the anxious frown at the blunt bombshell, Quilla rammed her message home, her mouth curling distastefully.

'Which means, as you will have guessed, that he now wants an affair with me and is more than willing to drop you. I'm sorry to put it so bluntly, but perhaps it will make you realise what a louse he actually is.'

'And you don't want an affair with him, I take it?' Marian stared at her as if she'd gone mad, groping for a chair and sitting down hurriedly, as if her legs were about to give way under her.

Quilla snapped tersely, 'Like hell I do!' then sat down, too, forcing herself to stay calm. Marian was acting strangely, but then, Quilla rationalised, she would be feeling awful, guilty because her infidelity had been found out and sickened because her lover, while openly admitting his affair with her, was more than willing to walk away the moment another woman took his fickle fancy. So, if there were to be any hope of saving her brother's marriage, now was the time to soft pedal.

So Quilla smiled ruefully into the bemused face opposite her and said honestly, 'I admit he's an attractive devil—far too attractive for his own good. And he's made his interest in me very plain since we met here——'

'I did notice,' Marian put in, smiling faintly, and, puzzled by this reaction, Quilla went on,

'To be painfully truthful, I discovered that he can make me respond the way no other man ever has. I could easily lose my head and wake up one morning to find he'd become my lover. The thought terrifies me.'

'Why?' The question was quietly put and it wasn't at all what Quilla had expected to hear; she'd expected hysterics, recriminations...

She frowned, but answered candidly, 'Because I wouldn't be able to live with myself if it happened. Well...' She shrugged slender shoulders. 'I could, I suppose, but I wouldn't like myself. I don't intend to be one in a line of suckers and I suppose I'm laughably old-fashioned, but when I make love with a man it will be because I love him and he loves me, because we respect each other. I won't go to bed with a man who'll change his women with as little thought as he changes his socks. I'd want everything—marriage, permanence—not a few stolen nights and furtive weekends.'

'And Fraser's not the marrying kind,' Marian responded thoughtfully. 'Oh, he makes no secret of it—he doesn't set out to deceive. The women he dates all know the score. He's not exactly afraid of emotional commitments, but he doesn't need them. I take it he hasn't actually proposed?'

'Not with a wedding-ring in his pocket and a promise of undying fidelity on his lips, no,' Quilla snapped scornfully. Leaving Marian to make what she would of that, she sipped at the scalding coffee and wondered why the conversation had taken this turn. She wasn't meant to be revealing her own fears about her inability to handle McGill, but trying to help Marian put the pieces of her marriage back together again.

So she pulled herself together and said staunchly, 'Forget McGill. You've got to try to save what's left of your marriage.'

And after a tiny shocked pause Marian whispered, 'I don't understand,' and Quilla said briskly, 'Then you'd better try. Jon knows about you and McGill. He put two and two together when he discovered that you and your boss weren't working late. And he didn't believe in the mythical old school friend you were supposedly spending this weekend with, either. But he did check up, giving you the benefit of the doubt, I suppose. He phoned the number you'd left, asking to speak to you, and the woman who answered said she'd never heard of you. So what happened?' she asked, her voice tightening with a driving need to know. And if she hadn't known better she would have attributed the pain inside her to jealousy. 'I suppose he joined you yesterday with some lame excuse or other? Or did he manage to get to where you were holed up late on Saturday night?'

'Jon knows?' Annoyingly, Marian ignored the question, her face going paper-white. 'Jon actually told you he thinks I'm having an affair with my boss?' Her eyes were wide and panic-stricken and suddenly Quilla felt her heart twist with pity—while not for a moment condoning what her sister-in-law had done. She herself had first-hand knowledge of how very tempting McGill could be, with his rough-velvet voice, sexy smile and fantastic body.

Poor Marian had probably been vulnerable; Jon had admitted that the marriage had been at a low ebb for months. She would have been a push-over for a sexy devil like McGill.

'I'm afraid so,' she admitted huskily, impulsively reaching out a hand to touch the other woman's. 'But I know he still loves you. If you could convince him that Fraser means nothing to you, that you won't see him again—even if it does mean you'll have to change your job——'

'Oh, Quilla!' Marian burst into tearful, hysterical laughter. 'Oh this is crazy!' She scrabbled in her skirt pocket for a handkerchief and scrubbed at her eyes. 'I think the world of Fraser McGill—he's great to work for, one of the kindest, cleverest men I know... But an affair? Such a thing would never occur to either of us. Besides, I'm in love with that stubborn, workaholic husband of mine.'

Under Quilla's incredulous eyes she took several noisy gulps of her coffee and, as if the dark brew had sobered her, said firmly, 'Jon's off his head if he thinks I'd ever look at another man.'

But Fraser McGill had more or less admitted to the affair—at least, he hadn't denied it—and Quilla had the evidence of her own eyes and, while she desperately wanted to believe what she'd just heard, she had to be sure.

'Before your dinner party I saw you coming out of his room. He was practically naked and you both looked—well, intimate.'

Just for a moment Marian looked blank and then she shrugged, 'Oh, that. I couldn't remember if there were any fresh towels in his bathroom, and Mrs Hodge couldn't, either. She was busy with dinner, and you know what a grouch she can be sometimes if anything upsets her, so I went to check. When you saw me coming out of his room he'd been trying to persuade me, yet again, to come clean with Jon, and I'd got upset—as usual, I'm afraid——'

'What do you mean—come clean?' Quilla interrupted, beginning to feel seriously out of her depth, and Marian shrugged miserably.

'About the clinic, of course. Only it's all turned into such a mess. And when I left this morning I phoned through to Cherry, just to see if Jon had been concerned or interested enough to try to get in touch, and she said he had, early on Saturday morning, only Cherry had gone down to the shops and her daily answered, and of course she didn't know who the hell Marian Kent was, did she? I thought, at the time, it was the best thing to do. I've know Cherry since our schooldays but we lost touch when she married a Welsh doctor and moved to Swansea and I asked her if I could give Jon her phone number, just in case he needed or wanted to get in touch. If he phones, I said, she could tell him where I was, break it gently. I didn't want him to phone the clinic directly, cold, as it were. It could have worried him. Only it all went wrong, and I think I've been stupid, only I was so worried, not thinking straight.'

'And not making a whole heap of sense,' Quilla replied, her patience running out. 'Why were you at a clinic? What clinic, for heaven's sake?'

Marian shrugged miserably. 'I suppose I'd better start at the beginning. You see, months ago, I started to think Jon was going off me. He's hardly ever at home these days and when he is he's exhausted——'

'He's building up the business, he wants to offer you all the security in the world,' Quilla defended, but added, 'Though I do think you should tell him how you feel. All couples need to spend time together and he doesn't really need to work all the hours God sends.'

Marian nodded, twisting her handkerchief to shreds. 'I thought he worked long hours to get away from me. We've neither of us talked enough, I suppose. I badly wanted a child.' Her voice was stark. 'But nothing happened, and Jon didn't seem to care.'

'But that's only because you're all he wants,' Quilla said compassionately, but Marian wasn't listening, needing to talk things through.

'I began to feel desperate. I'd always wanted children and thought if I could have a baby it would bring us close again. Anyway, Fraser discovered me crying into a filing cabinet one day and I poured the whole sorry story out. He suggested I went to a private clinic. He knew a consultant who attends one out near Hampstead. That was the start of the deception. I told Jon I was working late but I wasn't. Fraser took me to meet his friend then back to his home afterwards for supper, to calm me down, he said. Then there were other evenings when I had to go for tests and counselling, I used the excuse of working late——'

'But why didn't you tell Jon what you were doing?' Quilla interjected. 'He's been going through hell believing you were having an affair.'

'I couldn't,' Marian wailed. 'Don't you see? I believed there was something wrong with me, felt only half a woman. I couldn't tell him. And not only that, I was afraid that he'd tell me not to be a fool, tell me, again, that he didn't care whether we had children or not. In the state I was in I couldn't have handled that.'

'And this weekend?' Quilla asked, her mind whirling from what she had heard. Marian was telling the truth, there was no doubt about it. She'd never had an affair with McGill, so why hadn't he denied it?

'The same clinic. They wanted me in for a laparoscopy—basically, it's an investigation. My consultant told me this morning that there's nothing wrong, no reason why I shouldn't conceive.' Her eyes were misty with fresh tears, happy tears. 'He was so kind. He explained that my apparent inability to conceive stems from emotional tension...'

Turning off the Old Kent Road, she suddenly realised where she was.

She had driven from Marshbrook on automatic pilot. She had left home very early that morning, not bothering to make time for breakfast, and it was hunger pangs that were making her feel light-headed, almost euphoric.

She felt exhausted too, as if this morning's revelations had drained her of stamina, leaving her feeling like a bundle of disconnected nerve-endings, a creature of no substance—just chaotic confusions.

Once she'd come to terms with the startling fact that Fraser McGill had come nowhere near having an affair with her sister-in-law she had insisted that Marian phone Jon at work and ask him to come straight home. Only when she'd been sure that Jon was on his way and Marian was prepared to tell him the truth had she left herself.

Turning into the street where she lived, she became aware of the Lotus Elan turning behind her and her stomach lurched over. Fraser! She didn't know if she could cope with him right now.

Making a monumental and unprecedented hash of it, she parked in front of the red-brick Victorian house she shared with Nico, and Fraser slid in neatly behind her. She groaned, pushing her fingers through the long dark fall of her silky straight hair, flags of annoyance staining the pale skin that covered her high, slanting cheekbones.

She knew from bitter experience that she needed to be feeling one hundred and one per cent to cope with this dynamo of a man, and right now she was too confused to even try to suppress the involuntary shudder that slid over her body as he came to open the door at her side.

'I've been phoning all morning and all I got was the damned answering machine,' he bit out. 'Where were you?'

Mourning the poise that had been slipping ever since she had first set eyes on him, and which now seemed to be quite irretrievably lost, she scrambled out of her car, her wide mouth mutinously clamped shut.

He had no right to question her, to snap his annoyance because she hadn't been around when he'd finally decided to get in touch.

Hadn't she hung around all day yesterday, all evening, too, waiting for his call?

Then, horrified because she should think that of herself, when of course it wasn't true because she hadn't waited in for him to contact her—she had simply been at home, working—she tilted her chin in the air and looked at him down the length of her nose, her eyes narrowed to glittering golden slits.

'What was it you wanted?'

'You.' His voice was soft now, threaded with a rich sensuality that made her heartbeats quicken, and she had to grit her teeth and remind herself that he had no leverage now, not a shred of it, and couldn't make her do anything she didn't want to do.

'We'll have lunch,' he told her, grey eyes holding hers with an intimacy that shocked her. 'I know a quiet place by the river where the food's out of this world.'

She said quickly, decisively, 'You can't tell me what to do. You and Marian never did have an affair, so you don't have any threats to hold over my head. I don't have to see you if I don't want to.'

She held herself stiffly, expecting his anger because his bluff had been called, but she was wrong. The smile in his eyes touched his mouth and he just stood there, watching her, very cool.

Wearing narrow dark trousers and dark tie, a crisp white shirt, he looked as if he carried his own atmosphere around with him, as if the sweltering heat of the city on an airless early afternoon couldn't touch him.

'Then I'll have to make you want to see me, won't I?' He sounded very sure of himself, as if that would be no problem. 'Let's go. The table's booked and we've rather a lot to talk over, wouldn't you say?'

Witlessly, she followed him to the parked Lotus, pushing the hair away from her face with the back of her hand. She wished the heavens would open in a deluge of rain to cool the air, because the shaking of her limbs, the sickening feeling of something akin to excitement, had to be down to being over-heated and under-fed, and nothing at all to do with Fraser McGill.

And she was having lunch with him, just this once, to set the record straight. No other reason. She didn't want to see him ever again, not after today. He didn't have the leverage to make her, and she would tell him so.

Within half an hour they were sitting in a shady courtyard at the edge of the Thames. It was green and leafy, climbing white roses with their cool scented petals adding to the sense of tranquillity. There was even a tiny, river-wafted breeze, and the faint slap and suck of the water around the wooden piers was soothing.

They had been shown to a white-covered table near the water's edge, partially secluded from the other tables by a rose-covered trellis and as he ordered for them, intent on the huge, leather-bound menu, she caught herself studying his features as if she meant to stamp them on her memory for all time.

His insistent, assertive bone-structure was far more attractive than that of the most conventionally handsome man alive. His aggressive personality was impressed on the authoritative jawline, on the brooding slant of his cool clever eyes, on the openly sensual mouth.

Appalled by the direction of her thoughts, she dragged her eyes away from the inviting line of his lips and looked out across the slow-moving water to the houses on the opposite bank, half hidden between trees in heavy summer leaf.

'So you spent the morning with Marian,' Fraser stated. Having ordered, he was relaxing back in his chair, one arm hooked over the back of it, his cool eyes intent as though her reaction to his statement was important to him.

But Quilla wasn't going to succumb to the fatal charm that seemed to emanate from him in overwhelming waves. The way he looked at her as if, for him, no other woman existed made her feel giddy. But she didn't allow him even the smallest glimpse of that aggravating weakness of hers, and asked bluntly, 'Why did you lie? Why did you say you were Marian's lover?'

He smiled slowly, his eyes crinkling at the corners, very laid back. 'I never denied or confirmed your amazing assumption that I had seduced my PA away from her husband.' The smile widened, showing even white teeth. 'After all, why should I? I was very definitely the beneficiary of your wild imaginings.'

She wrinkled her brow at that, looking at him uncertainly, then pulled herself together and repeated snappily, 'I call that lying.'

'It is one way of looking at it,' he agreed suavely. 'But if I'd told you the truth you wouldn't have agreed to see me again. By deliberately setting out to lure me away from Marian, you'd already disgusted your virginal little soul. You saw me as the type of man who would foul his own nest by having an affair with a married employee.'

'You're disgusting!' she sniped, not sure whether her anger was occasioned by his blasé categorisation of what was permissible in a love-affair and what was not, or by his scathing reference to the virginity he must, somehow, have guessed at.

'Not at all.' He shrugged minimally. 'Simply a realist. And enough of a realist to have known that you wouldn't have agreed to see me again, under any circumstances, unless I had some means of making you. Because, for the first time I suspect, you'd become very aware of your own sexuality, and you couldn't bring yourself to admit that you were strongly attracted to a man you believed to have the morals of an alley cat.'

Quilla shot him a fulminating glare then looked away in confusion. How well he read her reactions. Too well. He wrong-footed her, left her with few, if any, defences.

'I allowed you to believe your lie,' he went on softly, the warmth in his voice making her stomach twist painfully. 'I needed that kind of leverage, just for a short time. I wanted to see you again. Very much.'

The arrival of their first course had her subsiding in her seat, her heart pattering with an energy that, an hour ago, she wouldn't have thought it capable of achieving.

The brute was so damnably sure of himself. He had encouraged her to believe a lie, playing games with her. But for her, and for Jon, it hadn't been a game at all.

When she thought of how she had wrestled with her natural fastidiousness, tossed her principles out of the window, when all the time he must have been laughing at her, enjoying the sense of power he got from manipulating her, she wanted to get up and walk away.

But the logistics of getting herself back to the city, coupled with her urgent hunger pangs, kept her where she was.

The pike mousse with Nantua sauce looked delicious and, giving in, she picked up a fork and didn't look up again until every morsel had vanished from her plate.

Ashamed of her weak capitulation, she shot him a guilt-stained look from beneath her thick, curling black lashes, but he was sampling the Taittinger the wine-waiter had poured, his eyes glinting at her over the rim of his glass, and as the waiter, at Fraser's nod of approval, filled her flute to the rim with the frothy, straw-coloured liquid Quilla decided to let her pride go hang, to enjoy the luxurious lunch she was being given and try to pretend McGill was somebody else.

But that wasn't easy. In fact it was impossible. He seemed, by some strange alchemy, to have garnered the magnetism of the entire male sex all to himself. She could understand why his amorous exploits were legendary. And he made it even harder for her to keep a sense of balance and distance when, over pheasant served with a rich gamey sauce, broccoli and buttered parsnips, he confessed, 'When Mari told me her problems I wanted to help. I introduced her to a friend of mine who does consultations through a private clinic. I had no idea, until Jon said something about my keeping his wife working late on odd evenings, that he wasn't fully in the picture. When I tackled her about it she refused to let Jon know what was happening. No doubt she had her reasons.' His eyes were dark, serious. 'I felt bad about it, but there was nothing I could usefully do or say. Outsiders don't help when they try to interfere in other people's marriages.' He topped up her glass, one eyebrow quizzically raised. 'Believe me?'

She did. It confirmed what Marian had already said and she could see her sister-in-law getting hysterical when Fraser tried to persuade her to tell her husband what was going on. Marian had believed he couldn't care less about having children and, in her overstrung state, had translated that into meaning that he didn't care about her, either, and that having to tell him she believed she was incapable of conceiving and was, in her own words, only half a woman, would make him think even less of her. But, hopefully, they would get things sorted out. They loved each other. And, with a certain amount of confidence, she crossed the pair of them off her list of worries.

Determined not to think about the other, more immediately pressing worry in the shape of Fraser McGill and his unwanted effect on her, she lifted her glass and drank, the champagne bubbles making her nose tingle, making her smile.

Fraser said huskily, 'You are utterly beautiful. And I want you. I think you're becoming an obsession.'

It wasn't said lightly and, despite the champagne, her mouth went dry. She said, 'Are you trying to tell me you're falling in love with me?' She had intended her remark as a flippancy, knowing full well his opinions on that particular emotion, but her voice had emerged huskily, almost as if she'd been pleading with him—which wasn't the case at all, of course it wasn't.

'Love?' He smiled at her, but his eyes were cold. 'I could say I loved walking in the rain or singing in my bath, but it wouldn't mean much, would it? It's an over-used word, Quilla. A pretty word. Tell me,' his smile was cruel now, emphasising the hardness of his facial bones, the coldness of his eyes, 'why do women need to dress such a basic, human physical need with pretty words? I told you the truth, as honestly as I know how. I want you, am obsessed by you.'

His eyes were dark, holding hers with an intensity that made her skin burn, touching some deep, unnamed core of feminine responsiveness inside her, drawing her, kicking and screaming, towards his inescapably potent male persona.

But that wasn't going to happen. He could impose his personality on every other woman he met, but not on her. Never on her!

Allowing him to bewitch her with his own brand of wicked magic would be the height of folly. And she wasn't a fool. Please God, she had the strength of will to keep herself from being drawn into the trap of his self-admitted obsession.

If she allowed herself to be seduced by him then her intuition told her that, for her, the magic would begin. He would enthral her, bind her, and she would never be able to let go.

But her beginning would be his ending. As he'd said, he didn't admit the emotion of love, the need for commitment and permanence into his life. The prey consumed, the hunter would move on in search of new quarry, a new pair of sparkling eyes, a new body, a new seduction. Obsessions didn't last, they quickly burned themselves out...

Sobering thoughts, but her determination to keep her distance didn't prevent her from enjoying the long, sybaritic lunch, his captivating wit, showing herself to be no slouch, either, when it came to intelligent, sparkling conversation.

It was half-past four when the Lotus drew up outside her home, and her heart was in her mouth, her pulses rattling, because she just knew, from the tension that had been building up—despite Vivaldi coming from the tape deck—that he would invite himself in, take her in his arms, and if that happened...

She turned to him, guardedly, and caught her breath when she recognised the smouldering, steamy desire in his eyes. And forced herself to say primly, 'Thanks for lunch. I enjoyed every moment of it. I won't be seeing you again, but——' and gasped at the shock of electrifying sensation as his hands reached for hers, took them and carried them to his lips, saying thickly,

'Don't fight it, Quilla. Now I've found you I've no intention of letting you go. Don't you understand? We were made for each other.'

He was slowly and surely drawing her closer, she could feel his body heat, smell the potent maleness of him, and the champagne she had drunk—he taking one glass only—was making her feel lightheaded, reckless, aware that any moment now the lips that were moving over her fingertips in openmouth eroticism would soon be covering her own, yet totally unable to do a thing to stop the natural progression...

A sharp rapping on the windscreen broke the spell and she looked up, her eyes hazy. Nico. Nico looking as flamboyantly handsome as only he could, was grinning down on them, wiggling the fingers of one hand, his lint-blond hair contrasting startlingly with the black jeans and shirt he was wearing.

'Naughty one!' he chided airily as she gathered her scattered wits and opened the door at her side, scrambling out on to the baking pavement. 'I've been searching everywhere for you. I thought the Martians had come to get you.' He glided away, using his key to open the grey-painted front door.

'Who the hell was that?' Fraser bit out.

Quilla dragged in a deep, unsteady breath, her heart banging against her ribs. This was her perfect let-out. A way to be rid of Fraser McGill and the threat he posed once and for all.

Despite his own inconstancies he would never share his women. A perfect let-out, and she took it. But her throat was stupidly tight and painful as she told him, 'Nico French. Don't let his vaguely camp mannerisms fool you. It's an act he puts on. For some unknown reason he thinks it's good for business. We live together. Didn't you know?' and watched, her foolish heart hurting, as his skin tightened over the hard, aggressive bones of his face before he gunned the engine and drove away, the sound of the growling motor and squealing tyres echoing through her mind long after he had disappeared from sight.

CHAPTER SIX

TURNING off the Via Nazionale, Quilla entered the hotel she and the team had been using while on the final leg of the Nico French winter collection tour. Tonight's show, the last, had been held in the ballroom of one of Rome's most prestigious hotels, the background of eighteenth-century tapestries, the huge rococo mirrors and glittering chandeliers emphasising, rather than detracting from, Nico's sleek and sophisticated twentieth-century creations.

The last three weeks had been a triumph, bringing rave receptions from cities as far apart as Glasgow and Paris, London and Venice, ending, as always, in Rome. And now the circus would be disbanding, most of the models moving on in the morning, back to home base or new assignments, Nico with them, she opting to take a few days' holiday, a well-earned rest from the frenzied activity of the last weeks, here in Rome, her favourite city.

The idea didn't give her the pleasure it should have done.

Sidestepping to avoid a group of residents, dressed up to the nines and obviously intent on sampling the glittering night-life of a city that never seemed to sleep, she saw a wide pair of shoulders, the back of a sleek dark head, and her heart stood still. Then thumped heavily on as the man turned and she saw his face. A perfectly ordinary face. Damn Fraser McGill!

During the six weeks since he'd taken himself out of her life he'd haunted her. She would never have thought it possible to miss the bastard so much. There had to be something wrong with her.

Her face set, her shoulders rigid beneath the sculptured heavy silk suit that exactly matched the colour of her eyes, she entered the lift and leaned wearily against the gleaming wood walls as it swept her upwards. She should be going down on her knees in gratitude. McGill's so-called 'obsession' had been mercifully short-lived and she should be over the moon about it.

Instead, all the could remember was that Sunday morning back in Southwark, two weeks after Fraser had driven away, his face hard with temper.

'Seen this?' Nico had passed one of the lurid tabloids he favoured over the breakfast table. 'You shouldn't have let your new boyfriend off the leash; he's found other skirts to sniff.'

'Don't be crude.' The retort was expected of her, so she had made it, but her mouth had tightened on a pain it was impossible to understand as she looked at the newsprint. The power-packed, lithe figure of Fraser astride a polo pony, bending over to kiss the outstretched hand of a dazzling blonde. The caption, 'City Financier with Constant Companion—and we Don't Mean the Pony!' said it all.

She had stood up, hiding the pain behind a stretched smile.

'I'll leave you to it. Some of us have to work if your winter collection is to be featured in glitzy shows rather than utter shambles.'

He had said quietly, tapping the paper she had discarded, 'You don't mind about this? You and he seemed a bit more than close. I thought he was about to take you in the front seat of that sexy motor of his. I did warn you.'

'Too much champagne on my part, and he's an incorrigible flirt,' she had dismissed scornfully, unable to bear his probing, intelligent eyes on her. 'Of course I don't mind. He means nothing to me.'

But she had minded. Still did, she thought tiredly as she let herself into her room. Minded too much, and it didn't make sense. He'd made an impression on her it was hard to shake off.

She'd hoped that the frenetic activity of touring the next winter collection around Europe would have helped her regain her perspective, put Fraser McGill and his alarming sexuality out of her head forever. But it hadn't. The ache inside her had become more intense.

Hormones, she decided edgily, stripping off the elegant suit, the wisps of satin and lace underwear. Either that or she was tireder than she knew, because no way had she ever wanted Fraser to become her lover.

Casual affairs weren't her style, she reminded herself for the umpteenth time as she stood beneath the shower. Had she given way to the undeniable sexual chemistry between them, taken him as her lover, then the only difference it would have made in the present scenario would have been one of time. The 'Constant Companion' would have had to wait her turn for just a little longer, that was all.

Fraser had the ability to switch his desires on and off like a tap. He never got emotionally involved, he had told her that much. And in that, at least, he had been honest.

Sick of herself and her inability to be nothing, but grateful because McGill had taken her statement that she lived with Nico in the way she had intended him to, she wrapped herself in the thick towelling robe provided by the management and walked out of the bathroom.

Nico was stretched out on her bed and she said, more snappily than she'd intended, 'What do you want?'

'To take you to dinner.' He smiled lazily, folding his arms behind his head. 'You should have waited, after the show. Absolutely heaps of orders, everyone raving!'

She didn't want to eat, to socialise with the others as they usually did, celebrating the end of another successful tour and endlessly chewing it over. But she had to make some attempt at normality, so she compromised, 'I'll eat with you, but not here. I'm not in the mood for the usual rave-up.'

'Anything to please.' He gave her a shrewd look, rolling to his feet. 'You need a rest. How long are you staying on here?'

'Three or four days.' But she wasn't enthusiastic. The magic of Rome, the Rome of Michelangelo, Bernini, Raphael, the city of winding alleys, ancient palaces, elegant shops and restaurants, had somehow lost its power to entrance. But that was her problem.

Sitting at the dressing-table, she began to stroke a brush through the thick length of her hair, changing the subject, her voice carefully light, 'And you? Where are you going to unwind?'

'Visiting my old mum in Eastbourne. She gets withdrawal symptoms if I don't show up from time to time.'

He was wearing tight white jeans and a scarlet satin shirt, the sleeves very full from the dropped shoulder-line, and Quilla pulled a face at him through the glass.

'If I were your mum I'd run a mile if I saw you coming. Now scoot while I get dressed. I'll see you in the bar in half an hour.'

Half an hour in which to unwind, to try to rid herself of the edgy, restless feeling that had dogged her for weeks, to get in the holiday mood . . .

She sucked in her breath at a rap on the door. Nico knocking? He usually just sauntered in. Maybe one of the models, come to say goodbye; several were booked on a late flight to London.

She pinned a smile on her face and opened the door. And froze. McGill.

He looked furious, his skin pulled back against his bones, his eyes hard and bitter. During the last six weeks she'd imagined she'd seen him in every crowd. And now he was here and the question sprang involuntarily from her lips. 'Why?'

He ignored that, cynical lines bracketing his taut mouth.

'Sharing, are you? Of course you are,' he answered himself, shouldering past her into the room. 'I practically bumped into wonder boy on his way out.' Steely eyes swept over her robed body and she felt herself flush.

She said thickly, her throat tight, 'Get out!' and saw his eyes fasten on the throbbing pulse-beat at the base of her neck and regretted her total loss of control.

Subconsciously, she had been looking for him everywhere, but now he was here she knew she couldn't cope. But she shouldn't have allowed him to see that, should have fought that instinctive command. It had been too revealing, letting him know that self-preservation was uppermost in her mind when he was around.

But too late to change that now. Already his eyes were glinting with awareness and he loosened the light grey tie he was wearing with the dark grey suit and white shirt, his eyes never leaving her face.

'We're both fools if we think we can fight it, Quilla,' he said huskily, moving towards her. Instinctively, she backed away, her eyes held, fascinated, on the softening line of his mouth as he told her, 'I've nearly bust a gut trying to put you out of my mind. Nothing works, not a damn thing. I gave up trying last night, got myself on a flight this morning. I want you, need you.'

No mention of love, she thought wildly. But there wouldn't be, would there? Not from this man. She took another step backwards and found herself against the door, knew she was trapped when he put his hands on either side of her head, his palms against the dark, smooth wood.

He was close enough for her to see the dark line of stubble on the hard sweep of his jaw, to see the silvery flecks of light deep in the grey eyes, to see the individual golden tips on the sweeping black lashes, close enough to kiss...

He was a sexy devil, irresistible, and if he'd said one word of love, of caring and commitment, then she knew, in a moment of shocking self-realisation, that she would have admitted...

'Don't,' she protested thickly, blanking out her dangerous thoughts, her heart thumping painfully against her ribs.

'Why the hell not?' he said toughly. 'It's what we both want,' and took her lips in a ruthless, demanding kiss that touched her body into frantic, clamouring life, the control she had always prided herself on deserting her, leaving her open to his marauding expertise.

And then, as if he sensed her body's betrayal, the desire that flooded hotly through her veins, his lips softened, coaxing now, seducing her, making excitement throb at her pulse-points.

Roughly, his hands dragged aside her robe, sliding down her silky skin, and she lifted her hands to push him away, a thick denial in her throat, but he lowered his head to her aroused breasts, the sensation more exquisite than anything she had ever known before as he closed his lips around one throbbing nipple.

She was lost, and she knew it. Knew, that from the very beginning he had touched some deep and hidden core of response within her. She had fought him, fought herself, but now the fighting was over, because no one could fight the inevitable. Her body had taken on a will of its own and her hands were deep in the thick dark hair on his head, her fingertips finding the hard scalp.

He said hoarsely, 'Why live with him when you could live with me? Don't tell me he can make you feel this way.'

Her fingers stilled and she dragged in a deep breath, her eyes very bright, his words making her feel cold. And she asked raggedly, knowing the answer, feeling self-disgust climb through her with shrivelling fingers, 'Are you asking me to be your live-in lady? Have an affair with you?'

'Why not? You live with him.' He lifted his head, his skin dark with desire, and she stared into his brooding eyes, her own a sharp, glittering gold, flinching when he said thickly, 'I can give you a hell of a sight more than he can, in every sense of the word. He's not worthy of you.'

Had she been open to propositions of that kind then she might have agreed with him. But unless she loved and was loved in return she'd be a virgin on her deathbed. So he could take his proposition and . . .

She hauled herself away from him, her face burning with a painful brand of self-loathing as she dragged the edges of her robe together. How could she have allowed her body to betray her principles, to respond to him like the wanton he believed her to be? She hated him for making her feel like a tramp.

'He's worth a dozen of you!' she snapped, her teeth meeting with a crash, and saw his face stiffen, his eyes darkening slits, a muscle jerking at the side of his jaw.

He turned away, suddenly, his shoulders rigid, and he asked her, his voice very tight, 'Do you love him?'

The room was very quiet, the closed double windows cutting out the sounds from the teeming square outside, and Quilla could hear the heavy beat of her heart. She moved softly to the far side of the room, putting distance between them, and, because she couldn't lie about something as important as loving another human being, she prevaricated, 'What would you know about love?'

'Nothing,' he bit out tersely. Then, turning, his face a hard mask, 'But I do know how much I want you, know how good we'd be together.'

On a wave of shame because she knew the truth of what he said, she snapped, 'Stop thinking you're God's gift and get out of here! I'm meeting Nico and I'm already late and, as I said, he's worth a dozen of you.' She felt like throwing something but settled for, 'Go harass the blonde you play polo with—your "Constant Companion" according to one of the more lurid rags!'

He closed the door quietly—she hadn't expected that, and when he had gone the silence was thick and frightening. Her emotions roiling, she dressed in loose black cotton trousers and a waist-cinching gold lamé top. Her hands were too unsteady to use make-up so she left her hair loose and stuffed her feet into gold kid mules, wondering how she could possibly get herself together enough to spend a quiet evening with Nico, holding the usual post-mortem on the past three weeks.

But she had to do it, of course. The bi-annual showing of his collections were a vital part of their business. She couldn't let him down, no matter how emotionally overcharged she felt. Her state was directly due to Fraser McGill, his shameful proposition, her primitive response to him.

Nico was in the bar, his lint-blond hair and scarlet shirt easy to pick out among those of the models who hadn't already left and a couple of dressers who would be on the same flight as Nico in the morning, their comfortable middle-aged bodies clothed in almost identical powder-blue figured

Crimplene suits making them stand out from the younger girls, all dressed to kill.

Thankfully, Nico spotted her at once, as if he'd been watching the arched doorway, and in moments he was at her side, tucking his hand under her elbow.

'Thought you'd stood me up. Let's go. Entertaining a giggle of model girls out for a good time gives me a headache.'

Quilla smiled thinly, agreeing with him, thankful for his supportive hand when a group of Italian youths out on the town flurried round a corner and almost knocked her to the pavement.

Apologies, wide white grins, appreciative looks from openly lustful black eyes, and Quilla felt Nico tug her away, his voice dry as he told her, 'Just be thankful I was with you, or they'd have pinched your bottom black and blue.'

They were soon in the winding alleyways of Trastevere, ducking into the small, family-run trattoria where Quilla preferred to eat. Good Roman cooking, gutsy red wine, tables looking out on to the frieze of a twelfth-century church, golden in the floodlight. Surely a place where she could relax, forget the degrading way she'd behaved in McGill's arms.

Settling at a small table for two, running her practised eye over the menu, she had her hopes ruined when Nico remarked offhandedly, 'McGill came into the bar while I was waiting for you. Looked as though he'd have liked to tear the place apart. Drinking very large whiskies. Did you know he was in Rome?'

'He doesn't send me a typewritten list of his current and future movements.' Quilla sidestepped the question and returned to the menu, tension making her body go rigid.

If McGill intended hanging around she was going to have to forgo her brief holiday, leave Rome. A thousand miles between them wouldn't be enough.

And Nico remarked, his voice dry, 'He hadn't been in the room for more than five minutes before Merla made a beeline for him, and you know what that means.'

Quilla did. They had used Merla Raines many times before, her tall supple model's body, stunningly beautiful features and mane of ash-blonde hair making her presence on the cat-walk, the clothes she wore, impossible to forget. Trouble was, she couldn't leave men alone, couldn't resist them; to her the male sex was like a drug.

Knowing McGill's track record, the outcome of a meeting between them was a foregone conclusion.

But why should she care? Quilla asked herself savagely as the pasta with a rich bacon and tomato sauce she'd ordered arrived. She'd turned his insulting offer of a live-in, temporary relationship down flat, so there was nothing to prevent him looking elsewhere. She had made it very clear that she didn't want him.

She shuddered, pushing her now unwanted food around her plate, honest enough to admit that he could make her want him. More than that, he didn't have to be around to make her body restless with need. He was in her head and that was all it took to produce the humiliating yearning sensation that had kept her edgy for weeks.

'Not hungry? I wonder why.' Trust Nico, who knew her so well, to notice her lack of appetite. And the wryly cynical look in his eyes told her that

he'd made a shrewd guess at the reason for it and
come up with the right answer.

She shrugged, drinking her wine, replacing the
glass on the table before answering carefully, trying
to put him off the track, 'Too tired, I suppose. It's
been a hectic year. I think I'll contact the airport
and see if I can get a seat on your flight tomorrow.
All I want to do is sleep, and I can do that just as
well at home.'

She hoped he believed her; she didn't want
anyone knowing how strongly and unreasonably
McGill affected her. Merla was returning to
England on Nico's flight tomorrow, with some of
the others, and McGill would have no trouble in
discovering that she, Quilla, planned to stay on for
a few days. Odds were he would hang around too,
and she couldn't cope with that.

He was becoming as much of an obsession with
her as he had claimed she was with him. The only
sensible thing to do was take herself out of his orbit.

'We should seriously consider getting you some
secretarial help.' Nico's eyes were thoughtful.
'You've got too much to cope with, you're burning
yourself out.'

'We'll talk it over some time,' Quilla agreed,
sipping wine, thankful that she'd successfully taken
his mind off her real reason for wanting to leave
Rome. Besides, a part-time secretary would be a
help. She could handle her job, she loved every
minute of it, but the paperwork often swamped her,
keeping her up until the small hours several nights
a week.

Nico was saying, 'If you're finished, I'll get you
back to the hotel; the night's still young by Roman

standards so, while you get some kip, I'll see what I can do about getting you on tomorrow's flight.'

Nico might be flippant, occasionally acid and always far too shrewd, but he was a good friend to have when one needed support, Quilla thought as he escorted her into the busy foyer of their hotel. Already she felt calmer, confident that she could leave the arrangements for tomorrow's flight home in his hands. Back in London she would be better able to put tonight's humiliating encounter with McGill out of her mind—there would be enough work to handle after the successful tour to keep her mind fully occupied, even if the devil himself tried to muscle in on her thoughts!

The spacious foyer was busy, people wandering through from the restaurants. Quilla spotted several of their team, the dressers yawning, ready for bed, the much younger model girls all set to live it up for a few more hours yet, going slightly over the top now the current job was over, the strict working regiment of a careful diet and early nights gratefully abandoned until they were back on the treadmill again.

But her smile faded abruptly as she glimpsed McGill in the crowd, his face tolerant as he bent his dark head to catch what Merla was saying. The stunning blonde model seemed to be trying to graft herself on to the hard length of his body and an anguishing stab of unadulterated jealousy made Quilla's face go white.

McGill had an arm around the girl's tiny waist; he had made a lot of headway in the couple of hours since they'd met, Quilla thought sourly. But, with Merla, that would be no problem. The girl was man-mad and McGill was more man than most.

But it wasn't her business what the bastard did, or with whom he did it, Quilla reminded herself tartly, deciding to head for her room before McGill spotted her. But she was too late. 'Caught you!' Merla screeched, her long beautiful legs almost tying themselves in knots as she pranced towards them, dragging McGill with her. 'Deserting us all, sloping off to be alone! Naughty little love-birds!'

Quilla felt sick, the sudden ice in McGill's eyes, the hard slashing line of his mouth more responsible than Merla's silly gush, and she heard Nico say, close to her ear, 'Silly bitch. Make yourself scarce; I'll handle this. The last thing we need is her telling the entire hotel we're an item.'

Quilla fled gratefully, her face burning. She knew she was being a coward. Running from McGill looked like becoming a habit. But she didn't care, she told herself as she got ready for bed. Better safe than sorry. That had always been one of Mrs Hodge's favourite sayings and at the thought of her brother's housekeeper, the woman she had known for most of her life, she smiled reluctantly.

One day, when the trauma produced by her unwanted feelings for Fraser McGill had been successfully put in their place—which was right out of her mind—she would be able to smile naturally again. It couldn't come soon enough!

Settling herself in the comfortable bed, she closed her eyes, making her mind a blank. If she allowed herself to think about this evening's events she wouldn't sleep at all.

And sleep was coming in dark warm waves when the phone at the side of the bed intruded shrilly. Groping for the receiver, she cursed under her breath. If it was McGill she would blast his eardrums!

But Nico's voice came quietly, 'Hope I didn't disturb you, but I thought you'd like to know—you're on tomorrow's flight. It's all arranged. Merla offered to swap her ticket with yours—surprise, surprise! And no prizes for guessing just why she's more than willing to stay on for a few more days. She's got her pretty little talons safely into our friend McGill, so it goes without saying he was around when we were arranging to make the swap. He looked like a pussycat who'd just been offered a big bowl of cream.'

CHAPTER SEVEN

QUILLA negotiated the trolley down the narrow aisles of the small supermarket. As usual, she had picked the one with contrary wheels, refusing to run in a straight line. Shopping wasn't her favourite occupation, but since she and Nico had been away for three weeks the fridge and cupboards needed re-stocking.

Resigning herself to a long wait, she took her place at the end of the check-out queue and wished her slight, niggling headache would disappear. After yesterday's flight from Rome she had slept deeply, only resurfacing when Nico had woken her at eleven this morning with a mug of tea, telling her, 'I'm off now—lucky old Eastbourne! I've checked at the warehouse and everything's smooth, and I've contacted a secretarial agency and they've promised to send someone round towards the end of the week. But I should be back by then; I can only stand so much of dear old Mum's bridge-playing cronies. Everything's under control, so take a couple of days off and rest up. See you.'

At least she'd removed herself from McGill's dangerous orbit, she congratulated herself drearily, refusing to think of the way he would undoubtedly be amusing himself. It was no business of hers, and she didn't want to know, and her slight headache, the vague feeling of depression, was down to the weather. Sultry early August heat, a thunderstorm in the offing.

She'd bought more than she'd expected to, she realised, emerging from the shop, two bulky carriers weighing her down, sighing as an ominous rumble of thunder rattled overhead. She'd chosen to walk the half-mile to the local supermarket, thinking the exercise would do her good. And now, as the first few drops of rain soaked into the thin black cotton shirt she was wearing with a short colourful skirt, she bent her head and scurried along the pavement. Taxis didn't cruise this area and she'd get just as wet if she waited for a bus.

By the time she'd gone twenty yards the heavens had opened and the screech of tyres brought her head up. The gunmetal-grey Lotus Elan had slammed to a halt at the kerb just ahead of her and her heart missed a beat, then raced on, knocking against her ribs.

It simply couldn't be. But it was. Fraser leaned across the passenger-seat and opened the door.

'Get in.'

The rain was bouncing off pavements that half an hour ago had been baking in the sultry heat, silvery stair-rods plastering her hair to her scalp, moulding her clothes to her skin, soaking her feet. She couldn't get wetter if she tried.

'No.' She'd rather catch pneumonia than spend five minutes with him.

She lowered her head and squelched on, her face mutinous as she tried to shut out the unwanted memories of the way he had humiliated her back in Rome, the proposition he'd made, her own shameful response to his lovemaking.

And then a hand was gripping her arm in a band of steel, hustling her towards the waiting car. People who had been caught in the deluge scurried past, making for shelter, taking no notice. If she was being abducted then no one cared.

He tossed her bags into the back of the car, as if they weighed nothing, pushing her into the passenger-seat. She subsided, rubbing her arm. Tomorrow she would be black and blue.

As he got in beside her she glowered at him, her face flushed, and he bit out, 'Don't say it,' his eyes very dark. 'I can't stand stubborn women.'

Tough, she thought, staring straight ahead. What did he expect? He'd made a proposition any self-respecting woman would throw back in his face, and if he didn't like it he could lump it. And why wasn't he still in Rome, enjoying the delights of the ever-eager Merla? He must have got himself on a later flight yesterday. Mentally, she shrugged that aside; it was none of her business. She didn't care what he did with his time.

The car slid to a halt outside her front door and she scrambled out, her stomach tying itself in knots. Grabbing her bags with both hands, she muttered a sulky thanks and hurried across the streaming pavements, rooting in her shoulder bag for her door key.

'Let me.' He was right behind her, of course he was, he couldn't learn that he wasn't wanted, and he took the key from her, slotting it into the lock. 'Where's wonder boy? No, don't tell me,' he commanded tightly. 'He can be in hell for all I care.'

'He'll be back any minute,' she lied. She had told the truth when she'd said that she and Nico lived together. McGill had interpreted it the wrong way because that was how his mind worked, and she was glad of it—it gave her some protection. If he thought her lover was about to walk through the door he would take himself off.

But he didn't. He carried her shopping through to the kitchen and dumped it on the table.

'Get out of those wet things.' His eyes were hooded, sliding over her body where her wet clothes moulded themselves to every curve, and she caught her breath at what she saw on his face, her pulses already beginning to throb in unwilling response. But she gritted her teeth and managed coldly,

'I'll change when you're gone. Thanks for the lift.'

'I'm not going anywhere and if you don't take those things off I'll do it for you.'

She could see he meant it and, in any case, she wasn't brave enough to put it to the test. And she was down again inside ten minutes, dressed in old, well-washed jeans and a soft wool shirt, her hair rough-dried, tumbling around her face in a wild black cloud.

'Sit down.' He put a mug of steaming coffee in her hands and took a chair, straddling it, his eyes telling her nothing.

Quilla stayed on her feet; he couldn't tell her what to do in her own home. She wished he would go, she couldn't stand the tension much longer. Having him in the same room was asking for trouble. Already she could feel her blood heating with the desire that had lain dormant until he had come into her orbit, touching it to fiery life.

'I take it wonder boy hasn't offered to marry you,' McGill said flatly, his eyes never leaving her face.

She said, 'No,' sipping her coffee, almost smiling because Nico would have forty fits if he thought any woman was trying to tie him down to domesticity.

But any inclination to mirth quickly died the death when he said hardly, 'I'll marry you. If it's the only way I can have you, I'll marry you.'

He took her breath away. The insult, harshly delivered, didn't deserve a reply, but she said thickly, 'Get out of here. I wouldn't marry you if you were the last man alive.'

Hardly original, but it expressed her feelings, or the part of them she allowed to show. Something submerged told her that if he had mentioned love things might have been different, but that was something she wasn't prepared to think about. Not now. Not ever.

'You're going to have to.' He was on his feet now, his features taut. A very dangerous male animal. But Quilla stood her ground, her chin up. He was mad if he thought he could make her marry him.

Marry him! Once he'd slaked his physical lust, his burning obsession turning to cold dead ashes, she would never know where he was, who he was with. She'd be a fool if she settled for that kind of marriage; she wasn't crazy enough to walk into a living hell with her eyes wide open!

'Why?' she scorned, her long golden eyes blazing with challenge, and he closed the gap between them, gripping her shoulders with iron fingers.

'This,' he said, his voice thick and savage, and hauled her against the length of his body, taking her mouth with punitive possession, catching her off guard.

Quilla moaned, shaken by the grinding force of his passion, by her own quickfire, instinctive response. Her breasts were crushed against the hard wall of his chest and his hands were shaping her body and her arms curled up to hold him, aggression burning itself out, wild, fiery sensation taking its place.

Fraser groaned, his mouth gentling into kisses of unbelievable sweetness, and Quilla gave up, abandoning herself to the melting flow of ecstatic sensation.

His whole body was shaking with the intensity of physical need, a counterpoint of her own clamouring pulse-beats, and he lifted his head, his glittering eyes half closed as he asked her thickly, 'Does that answer your question?'

For a moment she was too shattered to speak, staring at him with blind eyes, her breath shallow and fast, making the tight globes of her breasts push against the soft fabric of her shirt.

He could always reach her on a physical level, he didn't even have to try. The attraction between them was an explosive chemical equation. But without love and caring it was worthless.

'It's not enough,' she told him, reaction to the way he had made her feel making her want to weep. She wished she had never set eyes on him. She hadn't had a second's peace since they had been introduced. Cursing Marian for making their meeting necessary in the first place, she said stiffly, 'Marriages without love don't work out.'

But she knew she hadn't got through to him when he answered blandly, 'My parents managed it. They didn't pretend undying devotion, but they rubbed along. They both had something the other wanted. He gave her security, a social position and a blank cheque. She gave him a son to inherit, made sure his home was run like oiled clockwork, a place fit for a king, and made a perfect and very beautiful hostess.'

And made a lousy mother, she tacked on in her head, shuddering. The example of his parents' sterile relationship, the total lack of love he had experienced as a child, had obviously soured him for life, created a blind spot. He had never known real love and so he didn't need it. What you'd never had you never missed.

She shook her head, her full mouth compressed. 'I'm not your mother. I'd need to love a man before I could begin to think of marrying him.' And stared at him defiantly, willing him to leave before she made an utter fool of herself and gave in to the insane and incomprehensible desire to burst into tears.

'Then you're going to have to alter your viewpoint,' he told her with quiet menace, his eyes icy. 'I'd have thought the recent farce between Jon and Marian would have put you off love for life. It's a dangerous emotion. Supposedly, they married for love—and look what happened. She deceived him, not physically, but mentally, and he immediately thought the worst of her; he couldn't accuse her of having an affair with me quick enough.'

It was precisely because they loved each other that the misunderstanding had happened. Love could make a person vulnerable, easily open to hurt and self-doubt. But it would be a waste of time trying to explain that to the hard man—he wouldn't begin to understand.

She turned away from him, her back dismissive as she began to unpack her shopping, putting the free-range chicken and long-life milk in the fridge and he bit out, 'Don't turn your back on me. I'm talking to you, woman!'

No man spoke to her that way. She straightened, her face flushed with anger. Controlling it, she clipped out loftily, 'As far as I'm concerned, the conversation's over.'

She watched his face harden, the bones standing out in stark prominence as he told her, 'It hasn't even begun. I asked you to be my wife and that's something no other woman can say. And, before you say another word, there's something you ought to know. I'm prepared to force you, if that's what it takes. I'm not giving you the chance to turn me down a second time. Once was enough and I'm prepared to make damn sure you don't do it to me twice.'

Her golden eyes wary, she stepped back defensively, as if he were offering her physical violence, and he said very slowly, very clearly, watching her taut features with eyes that didn't miss a trick, 'If you don't agree to marry me I'll ruin your brother. And don't think I couldn't,' he added softly as she dragged in a disbelieving breath. 'He's heavily committed in several areas, and over-committed as far as the south coast project is concerned. I only need to pull the rug from under his feet, turn down his request for finance, and he'll go under without a trace.'

'I don't believe you.' Her voice was thin, her heart banging against her ribs. He had the power to do as he'd stated but, surely, not even he could be so ruthless?

'You'd better.' His cold smile made her shiver. 'Don't forget, I'm in a position to know how close you and Jon are, what lengths you were prepared to go to in order to end my supposed affair with his wife.' He walked to the door then turned his head and looked at her coldly. 'You embarked on the game, and if you find the stakes are too high, tough. But the game's over now, and from here on in reality takes over.'

She dragged in a breath through pinched nostrils, her stomach churning sickeningly, her wide golden eyes riveted to his austere features, registering the tiny flecks of pure silver in the depths of his dark grey eyes, the cruelly mocking smile on his sensual male mouth as he told her,

'I'll leave you to break the news of our forthcoming marriage to wonder boy. And after you've done that I want you to move out. Go to Marshbrook if you can't think of anywhere else. I won't have my future wife shacking up with anyone. Be out of here before tonight or I'll break his neck.' He watched her coolly, his hand on the door. 'And don't even think of running to Jon, begging him to find another backer.'

She lifted her chin, her mouth tight, because doing just that had been her first, immediate reaction. And he smiled, slow and sure, as if he knew exactly what had been going on in her head, a tinge of derision in his voice as he elaborated, 'He's running to a tight schedule as it is; he doesn't have time to shop around for another backer, and even if he did I'd be fully prepared to block him at every turn—and don't for one moment think I couldn't.'

Very carefully, she punched in the numbers of Jon's office, her knuckles showing white through her skin as she gripped the receiver. She had grappled with the sickening implications of what McGill had said, long after he'd walked out of the door and now she had to speak to her brother, find out if Fraser McGill could break him, as he'd threatened.

'But he's away,' his secretary told her. 'Didn't you know?' Jilly Cox was a bright and bubbly girl; nothing ever seemed to faze her. 'It was ever so romantic—a trip to the Bahamas as a surprise birthday present for his wife—honeymoon suite and everything. I should know, I made the bookings! They won't be back for another week, and orders not to be disturbed, no matter what. Anything I can do to help?'

For a moment Quilla's mind went blank with frustration. The pressure she was under was something she couldn't confide to anyone. Then something clicked in her brain and she said quickly, 'Could I speak to the site manager?' Roger Campbell had been with the company for years, a shrewd, no-nonsense character. He would know whether the finance deal with the bank had gone through and just how important it was. Using sordid blackmail tactics to get what he wanted would come as second nature to the Fraser McGills of this world, and she had to be sure that the ace he had pulled out of his sleeve wasn't in fact a joker. For all she knew, the deal could have been finalised days ago, before Jon took off on a second honeymoon.

'I think he's around. He was at a meeting ten minutes ago, so he should be. Hang on while I check.'

The wait seemed interminable. Quilla chewed savagely on the corner of her lip, beginning to sweat, and she felt weak with relief when

Campbell's voice asked brusquely, 'What can I do for you, Miss Kent?'

'I'd like to know how the south coast project you're undertaking with Lionel Crane is progressing,' she told him, hoping she didn't sound as strung up as she felt. 'I'd have asked Jon, but it appears he and Marian took off on holiday while I was away.'

She had no fears that he would refuse to answer. He had known her since childhood and the fact that she took no part in the running of the company wouldn't deter him. As far as he was concerned, she was her father's daughter, and that was that.

'It isn't,' he replied shortly, his irritation showing through. 'We're still waiting for the go-ahead. I tell you frankly, we can't afford hold-ups like this.'

'Thanks, Roger, sorry to have bothered you.' She replaced the receiver; he'd told her all she needed to know. Fraser McGill was obviously holding back.

For long moments she sat at her desk, her head in her hands, fighting back nausea. There was only one thing that would make Fraser sign on the dotted line, she recognised bleakly. Much as the idea distressed her, she would have to agree to marry him.

She was ready when he came. After coming to terms with what she had to do her brain had gone very cold, every thought clear and simple, sharply etched.

As if she had access to his thought processes, she had known he would come tonight, if only to check up on her, ensure that she had done as he'd commanded, broken the news of their marriage to Nico, moved out, taken herself to Marshbrook.

She had dressed carefully, choosing a simple black skirt and a lightweight white wool sweater, pinning her hair back off her face. She looked cool and calm and in control, and that was the way she was, she reminded herself. She knew what she was dealing with and, for the first time since meeting him, she knew she could handle him.

She didn't even flinch when the doorbell rang, but let him in with perfect composure, showing him into the sitting-room, ignoring the hint of thunder in the dark grey eyes as he reminded her starkly, 'I thought I'd made it clear that I wanted you out of here.'

She sat down, inviting him to take the sofa on the opposite side of the coffee-table, her voice quite steady as she remarked, 'Surely that only applied if I'd agreed to marry you, and had broken the news to Nico?'

For a moment he looked shell-shocked, as if he'd been dealt a blow from an unforeseen direction and then he was back in control, his features like roughly hewn granite as he came back, 'You've had enough time to think of the consequences.'

'Of refusing your gallant proposal?' She took his point, crossing her ankles, her elegant legs shown to good effect in sheer black silk stockings. 'Of course. You've made an offer I can't refuse.' And saw the light come back into his eyes, one well-defined brow rising by a tiny, sardonic degree. 'However, I haven't told Nico. He's in Eastbourne, probably until the end of the week. That being so, I saw no reason to move out.'

'Then write him a letter,' he suggested smoothly, the shrewd assessment of his eyes informing her that he was taking his cue from her, playing it cool, playing it down, as if marriage arrangements, based on blackmail, happened every day of the week. 'The wedding will take place three weeks from today. Let me have a list of the guests you would like to attend and leave all the arrangements to me. You'll be married from Marshbrook, of course, and, naturally, I shall expect you to give up your job. You'll find being a wife and mother sufficient occupation.'

The thought of being the mother of his child brought a run of bright colour to her face, made a dent in her icy composure. But only a dent, and quickly patched over in the time it took to get up, go over to the drinks tray, pouring them both a Scotch. She needed it, even if he didn't.

He took the glass, raising it, the too-familiar sexy smile curving his mouth. She looked quickly away, not giving herself time to be affected. And heard him say, his tone very laid back, 'A toast, to us.'

'You may be premature.' She took her seat opposite him, holding his eyes with a hint of mocking defiance. 'I agree to marry you, but with certain provisos.'

He hadn't cornered the market on blackmail. Two could play that game, and she'd learned a lot from being around him. He'd used blackmail to get her to continue seeing him and the tactics had worked until Marian had told her that her affair with her boss had been a figment of Jon's jealous imagination. She was only amazed that instead of using the threat of ruining her brother's business to force her into becoming his lover he had gone the whole distance and insisted on marriage. He wasn't the marrying kind.

'And they are?' He didn't look worried, but why should he? He didn't know he was walking into a trap. This time she held the joker.

'I want a quiet, civil wedding. No fuss. And, directly after the ceremony, you will sign whatever it is you have to sign, that will make the finance Jon needs available.'

'You don't trust me an inch, do you?' he stated, and his eyes went black as she dipped her head in silent acknowledgement. She would as soon trust a homicidal maniac with a sharp knife.

'There are two sides to every agreement,' she reminded him levelly. 'Making the financial help Jon needs available happens to be your side of the bargain. Agreed?'

'Add your moving out of here well before French gets back to your side of the package,' Fraser insisted, 'and we have a deal.'

'Done.' Quilla's face was expressionless, giving nothing away. She had her own plans and was keeping them to herself; he would find out what they were soon enough.

But the look of intent in his eyes as he lifted his glass and drank to her made her stomach clench. His anger would be awesome when he discovered exactly what her plans were, his retribution unthinkable.

She swallowed the whisky quickly. So she wouldn't think about it now. Time enough to face up to it when it became inevitable.

'Congratulations,' Nico said drily. 'Though I must say, for a girl who's about to be married, you don't look exactly ecstatic.'

She'd heard the car on the gravel, assumed it was Fraser, so her nerves were on edge as she opened the door, and she said, more snappily than she intended, 'What are you doing here?' and he gave her a taut, humourless smile, raising one shoulder.

'I don't actually know. I got back from Eastbourne a couple of hours ago, found you'd moved out, found your letter telling me of your wedding plans and had the urge to come and see you. It seemed like a good idea at the time.'

Quilla expelled a pent-up breath and felt some of the tension ebb away. Nico looked unsure of himself, very unlike the laid-back, slightly cynical character she had come to know so well and when he said with a diffidence that sat ill on him, 'I admit Marshbrook's front doorstep is an elegant affair, but don't you think it might be easier to talk inside?' She admitted him reluctantly.

Fraser would be arriving at any moment; he was taking her to dinner and although she hadn't been wild about the idea she'd had to concede his point when he'd said they had things to talk about.

The wedding was only just over two weeks away and, even though the mere thought of it made her tense up like an over-coiled spring, she knew she had to show some interest in the plans he was making, if only to throw him off the scent. No way could she allow him to hazard the remotest guess as to the nature of her own, very private plans.

'Through here,' she said, opening the door to the sitting-room, and Nico followed, his eyes never leaving her, as if her pale face, the haunted look in her huge golden eyes, puzzled him.

He said, 'That's not one of mine,' meaning the neat fawn-coloured jersey silk dress she was wearing, and she shook her head, crossing the room to fix him a drink, unwilling to explain that by choosing to wear this particular garment—a rare impulse buy in a sale, and a glaring mistake—she had been making a private statement of uninterest. No way was she going to bother to make herself glamorous for her husband-to-be.

'Jon and Marian not home?' He took the small martini she gave him and began to prowl the room like a cat edgily familiarising itself to new surroundings and she watched him, her ears aching with the strain of listening for Fraser's arrival. He wouldn't be pleased to find Nico here, for obvious reasons, but she could cope with his punishing anger because she knew there would be worse to come once she had kept her side of the bargain and married him. Much, much worse.

'They're away,' she replied to his question. 'I don't even know if they'll be back in time for the wedding.'

Only the day before Jilly Cox had contacted her with a message from Jon, explaining that he and Marian were extending their holiday. And Jilly had tacked on, 'I don't blame him, in view of the continued hold-up over the south coast project. It's been years since he took more than the odd day off.' Which had only gone to consolidate her knowledge that that bastard, Fraser McGill, was sticking to his guns, refusing to make the necessary finance available until after the marriage ceremony.

'Tough,' Nico said spitefully, then swallowed his drink. 'And if you were thinking of sending me an invitation, don't bother. I don't want to actually witness you tying yourself to McGill for life.'

It was on the tip of Quilla's tongue to ask why he was so bitter, but she thought better of it because she already knew the answer. And she quickly reassured him, 'Just because I'm getting married, it doesn't mean I'm running out on you. I'll still work with you.' She would need her job—after her marriage she would need it more than ever—and she watched for the expected signs of relief, but Nico simply looked more petulant than ever.

But she didn't have time to work out why because she heard the unmistakable sound of Fraser's arrival and felt her stomach tie itself in knots.

She excused herself, the all-too-familiar turmoil she experienced whenever Fraser was around scrambling her brain. But she was outwardly in control as she opened the door to him, not allowing her tension to show even when he asked coldly, 'Who's here?'

His car was drawn up alongside Nico's BMW and before she had time to explain Nico said from right behind her, 'Just leaving. Two's company, know what I mean?' his voice dark with unmistakable innuendo, warming huskily as he took one of Quilla's hands and raised it to his lips. 'See you, sweetheart.'

'You won't, sunshine. Not if you know what's good for you,' Fraser bit out, and one look at the tensed muscles beneath his impeccable dark suiting made Quilla forget her astonishment over Nico's unprecedented caress. Her relationship with Nico was entirely platonic, always had been and always would be. But she had no intention of explaining that to Fraser. It didn't suit her plans.

However, she didn't want to see Nico plastered on the walls, so she said, her voice coming breathily,

'I'll be in touch,' and practically thrust her working partner through the door, banging it behind him, squaring up to Fraser, her eyes glinting.

'You don't own me yet, so don't try to act as if you do,' and, even knowing him, knowing what he was capable of, she was unprepared for the bitter savagery in his face as he told her gratingly,

'I'll act as I damn well please. And if wonder boy knows what's good for him he'll forget he ever knew you. He may still be in love with you, but you're going to be my wife, and the sooner he takes that on board, the better.'

Stifling the desire to laugh in his face, Quilla maintained a coolness she was far from feeling. Fraser's obsession with her was making him seethe with jealousy, bringing out a possessive streak in him that she had no intention of soothing away by telling him that, far from being in love with her, Nico's sole concern was to hang on to the business partnership. Let him suffer, as she had suffered when she'd seen him with Merla.

Hastily, she pushed that thought aside. It was too uncomfortable to live with; the admission that he could make her jealous was not something she wanted to dwell on. So she said with a cool politeness that made his eyes narrow, his mouth tighten to a thin white line, 'If you'll excuse me for a moment I'll fetch a coat, then we can go,' and felt his hand on her arm like a manacle as she turned towards the stairs, the droopy hems of the garment she had mistakenly thought such a bargain dragging around her calves.

'I've changed my mind; we'll eat here,' he said acidly. 'By wearing a dress that looks as if it's something your grandmother threw out ten years ago you've put me off the idea of enduring an intimate dinner for two—at least in public.'

So he had successfully picked up on her state of mind, she thought, resigning herself to several hours in his sole company. She would have far preferred the lively atmosphere of a well-patronised restaurant to his undiluted company, the tension, the sense of being on the knife-edge of emotional catastrophe that haunted her whenever she spent time alone with him. But by choosing to make a statement in her drab choice of dress, the unalluring way she'd scraped her hair back from her make-up-less face, she had spiked her own guns.

'Then if you'd like to help yourself to a drink, I'll see what I can rustle up,' she suggested, politely aloof, as if he were a complete stranger.

Only by mentally distancing herself could she hang on to her teetering self-control. If she allowed herself to remember just how he was blackmailing her she would go out of her mind. And she had to forcibly remind herself that she could be as devious as he, that proving it was only a matter of time, as she became aware that he was following her to the kitchen and not, as she had instructed, going peaceably to the sitting-room to pour himself that drink.

For the first time since moving from Southwark to Marshbrook she regretted that Jon had given his housekeeper time off, telling her to take a holiday while he and Marian were away. She hated being alone with Fraser; she wasn't sure she could handle it.

And she became even less sure when, after she'd assembled the ingredients for a Spanish omelette, he removed his suit jacket, rolled up his immaculate shirt sleeves and began to wash and slice onions, red peppers, and began relating the plans he'd made for their forthcoming wedding, sounding as though they were an ordinary couple discussing the details of a marriage they were both looking forward to.

It was to be a quiet affair, that had been one of the stipulations she'd made—just the four of them, Jon and Marian, herself and Fraser. And everything hinged on Jon's being there to sign the agreement for the release of funds directly after the ceremony, she recognised sickly as she reached the hot plates from the warming oven.

Jon wouldn't miss her wedding, she knew that, but his appearance depended on whether or not he got the message she'd sent to his Bahamian hotel in time. She passed the back of a shaking hand over her forehead and felt Fraser close up behind her, felt his hands on her shoulders.

Quilla stiffened immediately, fighting the treacherous instinct to let go, to lean against the warm, dominant strength of his body, and he said softly, 'Relax. Marrying me can't be that bad.' His supple fingers gentled her, kneading the knotted muscles, releasing the tension. And his voice was a warm drift of comfort as he told her, 'In fact, I think I can promise that the married state is something we're both going to enjoy.' He dropped a light kiss on the side of her neck and she quivered with unwilling response.

In this mood he was irresistible, but he wasn't pushing his advantage and, as if content to bide his time, he parked her in a chair, divided the omelette between the two plates and sat down himself, his slow smile lighting his eyes, warming her across the table.

He was the most devastatingly sexy man she had ever encountered, she thought, drowning under the impact of his eyes. And she couldn't even feel angry with herself for making the admission because it was the truth, and nothing could alter that, and if things had been different...

She felt too soft, too yielding to be capable of movement, almost as if, with his eyes, his smile, he had transported her to a dream-time where no one lived, no one mattered but this one man, and the look he gave her was warm and compassionate, as if he understood, as if he carried a map of her dream-time in his head, and one of his hands reached for hers across the table while the other extracted a small box from an inner pocket.

And before she could gather herself, understand what he was doing, she felt the coldness of metal around her finger and her bemused eyes slid down to focus on a glowing yellow diamond, set in heavy gold. Her heart constricted painfully, her emotions warring between the sensations engendered by the cold fire of the glittering stone and the warmly sensuous touch of the vibrantly masculine hand that held her own.

Just as, earlier, his fingers had manacled the soft flesh of her arm, his ring manacled her now. But coldly, almost impersonally, reminding her of what, only a few short moments ago, she had forgotten.

She hated him. Hated him for being so nearly the one man she could love with all the passion she had only recently, since meeting him, been aware she was capable of. Hated him for being flawed perfection, for the utterly ruthless streak that had made him see blackmail as a perfectly acceptable means of acquiring what he wanted.

Despising herself for allowing him to gentle her out of the intractable stand she had taken inside her head, for thawing her frozen emotions, she snatched her hand from his encircling fingers and removed the heavy ring, pushing it towards him across the table, saw the look in his eyes—which could have been pain but was more likely astonishment—and said coolly, 'I don't need that kind of gesture. A plain gold wedding-ring is all our bargain calls for. Anything else is empty show.'

He was having difficulty controlling his temper, she noted coldly as he stood up, pocketing the diamond. Through her grimly acquired and very necessary detachment she could see the furious beating of the pulse-points in his temples, the aggressive clench of his jaw. But the coldness in his voice outstripped her own as he told her, 'You don't give an inch, do you? You won't let yourself see the way things could be for us. But, by God, woman, I'll damn well show you. When you're my wife you'll beg for what you're spurning now.'

CHAPTER EIGHT

'You look beautiful,' Marian said, her eyes shining. 'It's Nico French, isn't it?'

'What else?' Quilla saw the other woman flinch at the coldness of her tone, but she couldn't do much about it. Ever since she had decided to marry Fraser she had felt as if she would never be warm again.

She gave an assessing, almost disinterested look at her reflected image. The pale topaz suit with its structured lines, aggressively padded shoulders and short straight skirt, worn with a pair of toning, spiky heels, not a flower in sight, made her look as if she knew exactly where she was going, what she was doing.

Power-dressing for her own wedding, she thought with a mental shudder.

It didn't feel like her wedding-day, and it wasn't, not really, she reminded herself staunchly. If she hadn't been able to keep that in mind she would have fled to the other side of the world long before now. She could only be thankful that Jon and Marian had returned the day before. 'We'd been island-hopping, incommunicado,' Jon had explained. 'I nearly had a heart attack thinking we'd miss the great day.'

'Jon said to tell you the car's ready. We don't want to be late.' Marian was beginning to fuss; she didn't like last minute hold-ups or brides-to-be who looked at the world from cold yellow eyes.

'I'm ready.' Swallowing a sudden and highly unwelcome lump in her throat, Quilla gave her sister-
in-law a hug. 'Thanks for everything, Mari, and
you look beautiful, too.'

Marian was wearing an ice-blue silk dress—it
emphasised her recently acquired tan and made the
most of her cuddlesome curves, and she smiled.
'Stop it, you'll make me cry!' And Quilla followed
her down the stairs and out of Marshbrook's main
door, chin up, shoulders straight.

In one hour's time she would be marrying Fraser
McGill. But it didn't worry her, not any more. Why
should it? She was going to give him a taste of his
own medicine, and she hoped it would choke him.

She'd seen very little of Fraser during the past
two weeks. Something to be thankful for. He'd kept
himself aloof, matching her mood, accepting the
sterility of their unenviable engagement. And his
absence, abroad on business, had given her a much
needed breathing-space, time to train her new secretary in to the intricacies of the job, finding the
girl not only willing but quick to learn, with some
worthwhile, innovative ideas of her own.

Jon had been frankly amazed by the suddenness
of her decision to marry Fraser, but Marian,
glowing more from her new-found happiness with
her husband than from any amount of sea air and
sunshine, had said complacently, 'I knew it was only
a matter of time. He fell in love with you at first
sight. I watched it happen, remember?'

A pretty thought, but monumentally untrue.
Quilla had let it ride, stifling the momentary
weakness of regret. He had always fascinated her,
right from day one. And later, when she'd got to
know him better, finding herself falling under the

spell of his undoubted charm, his dry wit, his warmth, she had almost fallen in love with him.

But she hadn't. Of course she hadn't. She'd had more sense. He was a ruthless, blackmailing womaniser and, physical attractions notwithstanding, he was a louse. And nice girls didn't fall in love with lice. They ground them under their heels.

She had pondered vexedly over the question of why he had insisted on marriage. Pondered until she'd thought her brain would burn itself out. He could just as easily, and with less hassle to himself, have blackmailed her into having an affair. Until one night the answer had come to her. Revenge.

She had, as he had admitted, become an obsession. He had asked her to have an affair with him and she had turned him down flat. Rejection was something he wasn't used to and his ego had demanded retribution. Hadn't he stated, when he'd told her of his intention to use blackmail, if he had to, to make sure she married him, that he wasn't prepared to give her the chance to turn him down a second time?

He would view the forced marriage as a punishment. Once his ring was on her finger he would, in his eyes, own her. Use her as he liked, make her pay for daring to arouse his desires and then refusing to satisfy them. There could be no worse punishment than that.

But revenge was a two-edged sword, she promised herself as the car drew to a halt outside the register office, and that was a lesson Fraser McGill was going to have to learn.

*   *   *

The wedding was quiet and soon over, and, when they emerged for the short drive to the exclusive restaurant where they were to lunch, just the four of them, Quilla didn't feel married at all, despite the unaccustomed heaviness of the wide gold wedding-ring on her finger.

In her choice of a civil wedding she had been adamant; she would not have been able to stand in church and make vows she had no intention of keeping. It would have seemed like blasphemy.

It was left to Marian to keep the conversation rolling, prattling away in the back of the car. Fraser had barely said two words, and Quilla less than that. Maybe, she thought, glinting a sideways look in the direction of his hard, humourless profile, he was as tense and overstrung as she.

Though she didn't see why he should be. As far as he knew at the moment his blackmailing attempts had paid off. He had got what he wanted, so why wasn't he gloating? She didn't think she'd ever understand him. Not that she wanted to, she reminded herself tartly. She wouldn't be around long enough, in any case.

The restaurant Fraser had chosen was unashamedly luxurious, the food and accompanying champagne superb. But Quilla was only interested in the document which, after a brief, sardonic smile in her direction, he placed on the table in front of Jon.

Producing a slim black fountain pen, Fraser added his boldly scrawled signature, his face a blank page as he invited Jon to do the same. And Quilla sank back in her chair, her long golden eyes clouded, wondering why the expected feeling of triumph eluded her.

But, for appearances' sake, she did her best to look contented with her new status. She made no attempt to portray ecstatic happiness, not even she could manage that. Congratulating herself that she had succeeded—Jon and Marian had stopped giving her puzzled looks—she raised her third glass of champagne and took a healthy sip.

She would hate her brother to know that she had only agreed to this marriage to ensure he got the financial backing he needed. He'd blow a fuse if he ever found out and she had no intention of telling him now.

If she could have contacted him earlier she probably would have done because he might, just might, have found a way out of the situation. But his site manager and his secretary had both confirmed the 'hold-ups', due, as Fraser himself had told her, to the way he'd been withholding the necessary funds. And she'd had to believe him when he had stated that Jon wouldn't have time to find another sympathetic financier. So telling him the truth would be unproductive and she would have to think up some sort of convincing explanation regarding her future behaviour. Quite what, she couldn't begin to imagine, not at the moment, she thought muzzily.

The champagne was vintage, utterly delicious—it seemed to fill a need and when Fraser stood up and extended a hand, saying, 'I think it's time I took my bride home, if you two will excuse a groom's natural impatience,' all she could do was float to her feet and giggle.

They were to spend tonight at the house in Belgravia, leaving early in the morning for their honeymoon. She didn't know where he had in mind. In a terse phone call a couple of days ago he'd said, 'Pack enough gear for two weeks. Nothing fancy.'

So she had, just for the look of it, and her case was at the end of the bed when he carried her up-stairs. She didn't know why he was carrying her; she was sure, well—almost—that she was capable of walking. And she didn't know why she wasn't objecting to being manhandled and couldn't be bothered to think it out. Besides, the sensation wasn't unpleasant. Quite the reverse. His arms were strong, making her feel safe and protected, and she could feel his body heat through the fine dark fabric of his suit jacket, hear the steady beat of his heart.

She snuggled her face closer into his chest and wound her arms around his neck. She knew he was horrible but, strangely, she didn't mind at all. She would have to try to solve that enigma later, when she didn't feel so floaty.

Being carried over the threshold of the bridal chamber was quite an experience, she decided, then giggled. And he put her gently down on the bed and she moaned a protest when he would have pulled away, suddenly decidedly reluctant to lose the body contact.

'Eager, Quilla?'

She opened her eyes very wide, trying to focus on the mysterious depths of his. Maybe she should feel insulted at that, but she didn't. He'd spoken softly, with a trace of warm humour, and that was nice. And maybe he'd spoken the truth, because wasn't eagerness the opposite of reluctance? And she was very reluctant indeed to let him go.

Firmly but gently, he unwound her arms from around his neck and stood back, his smile warm and wicked as he told her, 'You're delightful when you're silly on champagne, my darling. But when we make love I want you to be fully aware, every last one of your senses perfectly tuned.'

And then he began to undress her and she tried to help him but couldn't and lay back and let him get on with it, stripping her clothes from her body as if she were a floppy doll.

It was all very sexy, the most erotic experience she'd ever had and by the time the last scrap of silk had whispered away from her skin she was almost purring with pleasure, coils of melting, warm sensation building up inside her body.

'Sleep for a while, my darling.' He lifted one of her hands and placed his lips against the curling palm, and his voice was thick, unsteady as he covered her with the quilt and promised, 'I'll come to you later.'

And when he was gone she had never felt so alone in her life, or so lost, and she stared at the shining dark wood of the closed door, a breath away from tears, the ache of sexual frustration making her chew on her lip. She had wanted him to hold her, to make love to her, wanted it so very much. But he had gone.

She punched the pillow then dropped her dark head and went to sleep.

She came awake quickly. The tiny digital clock on the bedside table told her it was four o'clock. Calculating back, she knew she must have slept for well over an hour.

No longer floating, she was firmly back to earth and her mouth tightened with self-disgust. She had all but begged Fraser to make love to her, her inhibitions, her hatred of him drowned in a bottle of fine champagne. And wasn't that precisely what he had said he would do—make her beg?

As she got out of bed, her own nakedness made her stomach curl with embarrassment as she remembered how she had allowed him to undress her, had unashamedly enjoyed the process. He was probably downstairs now, rubbing his hands in anticipation, congratulating himself on yet another easy conquest.

He should be so lucky!

Quickly opening her suitcase, she rummaged for what she wanted and dressed hurriedly in jeans, a light sweater and flat-heeled shoes. She hadn't got much time.

Despite her earlier lapse, for which she roundly blamed the last three weeks of tension, her inability to eat breakfast or any of the delicious food at lunchtime, her unwise intake of alcohol, she had no intention of being Fraser's wife in anything other than name. And that for only as long as it took to get the marriage annulled.

Her heart beating thickly, her handbag clutched under her arm, she crept out into the corridor, closing the bedroom door carefully behind her. Thick carpet muffled the sound of her feet as she made her way to the head of the stairs.

No sound anywhere, nothing but the sonorous ticking of a clock somewhere. No sign of life. Maybe McGill had given the Williamses the day off. Her short upper lip curled derisively; he wouldn't want witnesses to rape. Not that there would have been any question of rape, just over an hour ago, the unwelcome thought came, making her face burn with bright colour.

Pushing the thought aside, she gritted her teeth and crept down the stairs. Suddenly, they seemed endless, the main door, across the spacious hall, a million miles away. But she made it, and the door-handle was smooth and cool beneath her hand and the hinges wouldn't screech and give her away because nothing would malfunction in any house Fraser owned.

'Going somewhere?' The tone was incisive, burning into her brain, and she froze, cursing her luck. She had meant to be well away before he discovered her defection, before he realised she'd beaten him at his own game.

'Home.' Turning to face him took all her courage, but she managed it, her chin high.

'This is your home.' Patience was thinly covering the cutting edge of steel. He had changed out of the elegantly styled lounge suit he'd worn for the wedding and the narrow black trousers and black open-necked shirt added an overtone of menace to the male sexuality that was such an intrinsic part of him. The hard line of his mouth didn't bode well, either.

'No,' she contradicted firmly. 'My home's in Southwark, with Nico. Has been for the past four years and will be for the forseeable future.'

'Like hell it is,' he bit out, moving closer. He looked as if he wanted to kill her.

She didn't flinch, even though every instinct told her to turn and run. He would overtake her with no trouble at all, haul her back. She had to hold on to her dignity.

'You're my wife. Where I live, you live. Where I go, you go.' His voice cracked like a whip, making her blood turn to ice, and now was the time to tell him the truth, if he hadn't already guessed it. Heaven knew, he was astute enough.

'We made a bargain.' Annoyingly, there was a break in her voice she couldn't quite control, and she swallowed jerkily and forced herself on. 'I agreed to marry you if you released the funds Jon needed. It was you who'd threatened to ruin him, if you remember.' She lifted her chin, finding the courage from somewhere, her eyes very bright. 'So I married you, kept my side of the bargain. I never promised to stay with you. I'm afraid it's a case of the biter bit.'

This should have been her moment of triumph, the moment she'd held in her mind ever since she'd known that, for her brother's sake, she had to marry the bastard. It was the only thing that had kept her from tearing her hair out at the roots during the past three weeks.

Revenge had a bitter taste and there wasn't even the tiniest flicker of triumph in sight. And, looking at his tight, furious features, the sudden dark bleakness of his eyes, she felt her heart constrict, almost as if it was breaking, and that didn't make any kind of sense.

But the moment of silent regret was over as soon as he took her arm, his fingers biting into her flesh, his face a mask of fury as he ground out, 'I should have taken advantage of what was on offer barely an hour ago; you were begging for it. I'd have wiped your memory clean of wonder boy, and that's a guarantee. You wouldn't have known what had hit you, I promise.'

She didn't know she had struck him until she heard the crack as her hand connected with his jaw and she saw his eyes narrow, black now, cold and fathomless, and his mouth was a thin slash as he told her, 'Don't ever do that again. Next time I might hit you back. And don't even think of going back to French. I'll wring his pretty neck if you do.'

Defiance was one thing, putting her neck and Nico's into a noose was another, and her eyes fell beneath his long, hard stare, her heart pounding as if she'd just run a mile.

And then her wrist was taken in a grip of steel and she was being pulled deeper into the hall, almost running as she tried to keep up with his long, impatient stride, colliding with him as he stopped to pick up the house phone, snapping out,

'Bring the Lotus to the door, Williams. Now. And ask Maggie to come through.'

The couple were probably relaxing in their own quarters, fancifully imagining their employer and his new wife engrossed in each other in the best romantic tradition. Nothing could be further from the truth, and his sudden, bitten-out commands must have come as quite a shock.

But his temper and tone had moderated by the time Maggie came pushing through the green baize door, although his grip on her wrist hadn't, the pressure becoming harder, if anything, as the housekeeper showed her surprised face.

It was as if he was warning her against making any kind of scene. He didn't know her at all if he thought she would do her dirty laundry in public, and she gave him a limpid smile, to prove her point, and felt his grip relax just fractionally, all the hard edges smoothed from his voice as he told the older woman, 'We've changed our minds, Maggie. We'll be leaving tonight instead of in the morning. If you'd fetch my wife's case from our room, and mine—you'll find it in the dressing-room—I'd be grateful.'

But the hard edges were back in full force as soon as the housekeeper was out of earshot.

'You've spiked your own guns as far as I'm concerned, my darling. From now on I'm not letting you out of my sight.'

His tone was nasty and so were the implications. He would use force to make her stay with him if he had to and the pressure mounted inside her head until she thought it would burst.

He wouldn't resort to rape, of course he wouldn't, Quilla consoled herself desperately as the Lotus ate the miles. During the last quarter of an hour it had become obvious where they were heading. Old Ford. Although he hadn't said a word, maintaining a tight-lipped silence, she recognised the terrain.

Being holed up with him in an isolated country cottage wasn't her idea of happiness right now. A hotel somewhere, people around, and she would have felt easier. Alone with him, no one else in sight, was a frightening prospect. An angry man could do crazy things and he was angry; the waves of rage coming off him were storm force.

She didn't blame him for feeling that way, she admitted with miserable honesty. Not only had she been on the point of walking out on him, a few hours after their marriage, but she had deliberately led him to believe that Nico was her lover, told him she was going back to him.

No red-blooded male would take that without some form of retaliation, and Fraser McGill was more red-blooded than most. What he owned he kept, and because he'd married her he owned her. His mind would work that way.

He must have arranged for some furniture to be installed, she thought, trying to calm her mounting agitation as Fraser put the car over the narrow bridge at a speed which had her catching her breath, wondering if they were about to take off.

And as he slammed the brakes on outside the gate, he broke his silence, telling her tersely, 'Don't worry, mod cons have been installed. There's no need to look so bloody apprehensive.'

That her apprehension was entirely down to him she didn't deign to tell him, but let herself out of the car and stalked up the narrow path, waiting, her face set, for him to follow.

The interior was a revelation, but there was far too much tension between them for her even to begin to think of telling him that. During the weeks since she had seen the cottage for the first time he must have employed a team of craftsmen, working flat out.

The place had been sympathetically restored, no doubt about it, cosy and comfortable, the antiques not show pieces but looking as if they had been part of family life for hundreds of years, lovingly appreciated and cared for, the fabrics and rugs, even the pictures and ornamental pieces, fitting the character of the place.

Turning in the open doorway that led to the charming sitting-room, she met his eyes. He was standing in the small square hallway, both cases in his hands, and her heart missed a beat.

'I'll take these to our room,' he said, tight-lipped. 'Coming?'

'You go ahead,' she dismissed, wandering through into the sitting-room, affecting uninterest. Her heart was beating like a drum, but he wasn't to know that, of course; let him think she was cool and hard, totally unaffected by anything he did or said. No way was she going into any bedroom with him. If he wanted her there he'd have to hit her over the head and drag her up.

Pacing the floor, her arms wrapped around her body, she regretted having mentally sympathised with his anger, recognising the reason for it. Whatever happened, she must never allow herself to weaken. He deserved all the aggro she could give him. By blackmailing her into marriage he had brought it on his own head.

The sound of his footsteps overhead made her shudder, and she scurried through to the kitchen. When she had been here before the room had been squalid, but now the quarry-tiled floor was clean and shining, bright geranium-red curtains at the windows, pine cupboards around the walls, gleaming work surfaces and a state-of-the-art electric cooker.

She wouldn't have been human if she hadn't been impressed by what had been achieved in such a relatively short space of time and, out of interest, she peered into the fridge, her eyebrows rising as she noted the smoked salmon, champagne, man-sized slabs of steak, Brie, fresh vegetables in abundance.

Everything had been laid on; he had obviously planned to make their honeymoon at Old Ford not only intimate but luxurious. Unwillingly, she remembered how excited he'd seemed when he had brought her out here that first time, the pleasure he'd taken in showing her round, in telling her of his plans to make this the first real home he'd ever had.

His throwaway remarks about his earlier life had been the first real insight into his character he'd given her. And she recalled how her sympathies had been stirred, how she'd found herself really enjoying his company, despite thinking, as she had done at that time, that he was having an affair with her brother's wife.

There had always been a deep, primitive awareness between them and it had been here, at Old Ford, that it had first flared into vivid life. Here, in the deep green shade at the side of the brook, he had given her notice of his intention to possess her, and it had been here, too, that she had wondered dazedly if she was falling in love with him.

Recognising the dangerous paths her reverie had led her on to, she squared her shoulders, marched over to the outer door, slid back the bolts and walked out into the tangled garden, drowsing in the dusty dry warmth of the August evening.

And right behind her Fraser said, 'It's a beautiful evening. If you're taking a walk I'll come with you.'

She dragged in her breath, not turning, her shoulders rigid. He had developed a habit of creeping up on her when she least wanted him around, taking her unawares, unprotected by the cold cloak of indifference that was her best defence. And she said, 'If you like,' robbed of a snappy come-back by the unexpected warmth of his tone.

'Know anything about gardening?' His arm, draped loosely around her shoulders, made her spine go stiff, but she answered his question at face value because the evening was too peaceful and perfect to spoil with the snapping and snarling that had become their normal dialogue recently. For some reason she hadn't the heart for it.

'A bit. I used to potter about helping Mother at Marshbrook when she was alive. She was very keen and, I think, quite knowledgeable about plants.' Spending long hours in the garden with her mother had been one of the many things she'd missed. Her father, up until the tragic death of his wife, had taken an interest. Afterwards he'd turned his back on it, as he'd turned his back on his children, employing a gardener, never going near the lawns and flowerbeds his wife had created again.

Fraser's hand tightened briefly on her shoulder, as if he had picked up the nostalgic wistfulness of her tone, and he said, as if it mattered, 'Good. I'd like to turn this jungle into a real old-time cottage garden but haven't the least idea how to begin. So you can shout out instructions and I'll supply the muscle power. How does that grab you?'

He was smiling, she could hear it in his voice, and he was talking as if he thought they had a future together, which was strangely sad because hadn't she made it quite clear that her first priority was to end the marriage he'd so ruthlessly forced her into?

'And over there,' he gestured towards a stand of dusty old conifers that looked particularly out of place, 'I thought we might get those felled, make somewhere safe for children to play, shallow paddling-pool, sandpit, a miniature log cabin that could be used as a play-house.'

They had been walking slowly in the direction of the brook and his calm assumption that they should have children together made her go weak at the knees. Weak all over. And if, somehow, his arm hadn't slipped down to her waist, supporting her, she would have fallen.

As it was, his hand tightened around her waist, bringing her much closer to the lean strength of his body, and she knew if she tried to move away he would simply haul her back.

Weakly, she allowed him to take her into the clearing where they'd picnicked that day—how long ago it seemed, wondering where his anger had gone. The cold rage that had possessed him since she had told him she was leaving him, returning to Southwark, had never intended to stay with him, had, incomprehensibly, disappeared. She didn't think she'd ever understand him, get to know what motivated him. He was complex and tricky and she should be stamping back to the cottage, locking herself in one of the bedrooms and planning how to get away.

But she wasn't. She was standing with him at the stream's edge, watching the green glimmer of water. The evening sun, piercing the overhead canopy of leaves, touched the dancing surface here and there with brilliant pin-points of light. And he said softly, 'It's beautiful, isn't it? Peaceful. You feel you can breathe properly.'

It was peaceful, no traffic noise, no exhaust fumes, no hassle. No hassle?

She wondered why, suddenly, the tension that had been winding her up ever since he had threatened to ruin her brother if she refused to marry him had left her. Wondered why she wasn't planning to get away from here at the earliest possible opportunity. Was it because her intuition told her that this was not the time to run, that she had to stay, for a while at least, try to face up to the attraction—unwilling on her part—that she and Fraser shared?

She simply didn't know, and before she had time to analyse her motives he turned her to face him. Just the lightest pressure of his hands was enough to position her in the warm circle of his arms and there were dancing glints of silvery light in his eyes, too, a warmth in the sensual curve of his mouth that she found disarming.

'And the scenery's not the only beautiful thing around here,' he told her, his hands moving to cup her face. 'You're exquisite.' He looked relaxed, his mouth softening in a smile that took her breath away. Her heartbeats quickened; when he was in this mood he could make her melt.

The black shirt he wore was open at the neck, revealing the corded strength of his throat, the olive-toned skin. And he moved closer, increasing the pressure of his body against hers, and she saw his eyes darken as her breasts pushed against the thin fabric that covered his chest.

Her breath came rapidly, the tension mounting inside her again. A different kind of tension, she recognised, sexual tension. And she shouldn't be standing here letting it happen, she knew she shouldn't, but found she couldn't move away, no matter how insistently the small, still-functioning part of her mind told her to.

Only he had the power to do this to her, to make her melt, the power to turn her into a creature of wanton needs, desires she had never known existed until he had conjured them forth with his voice, his eyes, his hands, his body.

Quilla moaned softly, halfway between self-disgust and elemental need, and he took her breath into his mouth, closing his persuasive lips over hers, and she was lost.

Slowly he lowered her to the ground, to the sweet soft grass, and he was breathing deeply, roughly. She looked up at him, saw raw, primeval need on his face, a yearning that cried out to the unfurling response that had begun deep within her, a response that ached to be met. And as the twilight deepened, painting his face with mystery, she said his name, just once, and held out her arms to embrace him. Something that had no name was born inside her, some ageless knowledge that told her all she needed to know.

She loved him. She had loved him all along and had been too blind to recognise what fate had offered her in the irresistible shape of Fraser McGill.

CHAPTER NINE

EVERYTHING was different in the morning. Perhaps it always was. Perhaps that was the way of the world. Or the way of men.

When she woke to dawn light and birdsong, snug in the big double bed with Fraser deeply asleep at her side, on his back, the fine linen sheets tangled around his long, hair-darkened legs, Quilla didn't know that everything had changed, was different, of course she didn't. She wasn't to know that until much later.

After their first, ecstatic lovemaking he had carried her indoors. Neither had thought of food, only of each other, and he had swept her upstairs, to the big double bed in the master bedroom, and had initiated her into the deeper delights of loving fulfilment, teaching her to pleasure him as he pleasured her, taking her with him to the distant planets, bringing her down again gently at last, to sleep safely beside him, dreaming of him.

It was far too early to wake him, yet she knew she would if she stayed. Kiss the sleep-softened planes of his face to wakefulness, watch the brooding grey eyes open to the light and to her.

Tempting though that thought was, he needed to sleep and she needed to think. Think of what had happened to her, of falling in love. Of loving.

She got quietly out of bed and went through to the bathroom and showered. The smoked glass shelves were well stocked with very feminine, outrageously expensive toiletries and her heart turned to mush. He had bought them specifically for her use, spoiling her. He most certainly hadn't chosen them for himself!

And because she was feeling very feminine, very romantic, she used them liberally then dressed herself in a full, honey-coloured swirling skirt, teaming it with a front buttoned sleeveless black silk blouse that clung very lovingly indeed, leaving more buttons undone than was modest.

But she wasn't feeling modest, far from it, and after checking that Fraser was still asleep she padded outside, the dew on the grass making her bare feet tingle. She breathed in deeply, taking the fresh fragrant air down into her lungs. Later, perhaps, they would begin to make plans for the garden—already she could see the play area he'd spoken of, the children, looking like him. And she wanted, she found, to have his children, wanted it badly. It was a part of her love for him.

Loving him had implications beyond her willingness to accept the marriage, to stay with him always. And it was that she had to think of. One day. This morning her thoughts were elusive, like brightly coloured butterflies, there, but always beyond reach, impossible to pin down.

And perhaps she deserved this day of freedom from thought, a day given over to the wonder of falling in love. Time enough to tell him how she felt later, to discuss their future, to come to terms with the tactics he had used to get her to marry him in the first place, with his own inability to admit love, with all its dependencies, into his heart.

And she, in turn, would have to make him believe that she and Nico had never been lovers, that, indeed, she had taken no lover, ever, that he had been the first and he would be the last.

He wouldn't have been able to tell she was a virgin, of course—had he done it would have solved a lot of problems, reinforced the truth of her platonic relationship with her business partner. But there had always been ponies at Marshbrook in her childhood and she had ridden a great deal, right into her late teens, and that, so she had heard, made a difference.

So today she would simply enjoy the flowering of love... She turned back to the house, investigated the kitchen to find where everything was kept.

Places laid at the small pine table, strips of bacon and tomatoes ready to go under the grill and the coffee gurgling in the filter machine, she heard him move around upstairs and her heart leapt with pleasure.

And his coffee was already poured and waiting when he walked into the room. He was freshly shaved and showered, dressed in a well-washed T-shirt that displayed the wide rangy width of his shoulders and a pair of old denims that left his masculinity in no doubt at all and made her veins run with fire, her cheeks turn distinctly rosy.

'What got you up so early; couldn't you sleep?'

There was a note of cynicism in his voice that she didn't understand at all. Surely he didn't think, not after last night, that she still intended to walk out on him? She would have to show him that nothing was further from her mind now.

So she smiled into his eyes. 'Drink your coffee,' she said, and slid the bacon under the grill. 'I was awake. It was such a lovely morning, I didn't want to waste it lying in bed.'

'So you class lying in bed with me as a waste of time? Hardly a flattering admission for a new bride to make. I must be losing my touch. After your response to me last night I was beginning to hope...' he shrugged. 'But only fools live on hope, don't they?'

He smiled, but there was no humour in it, none at all, and Quilla frowned as she turned the bacon. He had taken her the wrong way. Deliberately? And she didn't like the oblique reference to the other women who had shared his bed in the past and who, no doubt, had been most reluctant to leave it.

She couldn't tell him the truth, that she had had to force herself away, denying her instinct to wake him with kisses, needing a few quiet minutes to privately examine the wonderful newness of her love for him. He didn't love her, he had shut his mind to the possibility of loving anyone, and the way he had been brought up had been responsible for that. He had told her he didn't know what love was, implying it was just a pretty word used by fools. To tell him she loved him would embarrass and annoy him.

So she divided the food between two plates and brought them to the table where he was sitting, drinking coffee, and pinned a bright smile to her face,

'I don't want to start a fight!' Her golden eyes were smiling and soft as she sat opposite him, soft with love, but they glittered with the sudden sting of unshed tears when he said nastily,

'That makes a change. It's been all you've ever wanted to do with me until now.'

And whose fault was that? Her mouth clamped into a mutinous line. Right from the start he'd made his intention to possess her quite clear, using threats and blackmail to get what he wanted. Had he really expected her to give in without a fight? Especially once she'd learned that he been regularly dating the blonde he'd been pictured with at that polo match!

Fraser had finished his breakfast, but she hadn't been able to eat a thing. His attitude, following the passion of last night, had tied her stomach in knots.

'Not hungry?' He helped himself to more coffee and put his arms on the table, his eyes drifting over her. 'You look remarkably fetching this morning, my darling.' His message of intent was clear to read and tiny fingers of sensation tingled over her skin as he put out a hand and traced a slow line between her breasts, deftly undoing even more of the tiny buttons.

Quilla pulled in her breath, feeling her eyes grow heavy with desire, and as they closed, long lashes drifting down, she heard him say softly, 'I can always reach you this way, can't I? Whatever else happens, we'll always have this.'

He had exposed both naked breasts now and came to stand behind her, sliding his hands over her shoulders, down to cup the shamelessly aroused peaks. And she knew he was right, he could always reach her this way, and she wasn't fighting him, not any more.

She loved him, wanted him, and when he pulled her to her feet, turned her in her arms, she went willingly, winding her arms around his neck and pulling his head down, waiting for his kiss. But he said, 'I promised you'd forget wonder boy, didn't I, my darling? I guarantee you haven't given him a single thought since I first took you.'

Her wide eyes stared into his. She was thrown off balance at first by his cynical reference to Nico French, but her heart twisted with sudden compassion. Since he'd woken to find her missing from his bed he must have been brooding on her supposed sexual relationship with Nico. And that would have been responsible for his bitter mood. It was all her fault, she thought guiltily. She had used the fact that she and Nico shared a house in self-defence, had implied that they were lovers. Somehow she was going to have to convince him otherwise, but he said sarcastically, 'Don't worry about it. Just keep it that way.'

Now was the time to put him straight about the true state of her relationship with Nico; she didn't want him harbouring unnecessary grudges and jealousies. Looking deep into his shadowed eyes, she told him, 'Nico's a business partner, nothing more. I've never been to bed with him.'

But she felt the sudden rigidity of his body as he said tonelessly, 'Don't lie to me. Only a fool would believe that. You've been living with the bastard for four years and you've already admitted to an affair.' His arms tightened savagely around her, pulling her into the hard length of his body and, his mouth a whisper away, he told her brutally, 'I refuse to discuss it. He no longer exists, for me or for you. Keep it that way or you won't know what's hit you,' and took her lips with his, demanding submission.

She hoped things would change. She hoped quite desperately. And sometimes she thought they would and sometimes she knew they couldn't.

Her emotions on a see-saw, she lived from day to day, not knowing what the next moment would bring. His mood changes were frightening. But there was always passion, there was always that, and she told herself staunchly that, for the time being, it was enough. It would have to be. Longing for more than he could give of himself wouldn't cure anything.

The dog days of summer trickled by, the air dusty with heat, the evenings misty with the faintly melancholy foretaste of autumn, of the end of things.

But working in the garden, at least, was unshadowed happiness. They made a good team, found plenty to discuss, plenty to laugh about. Fraser knew what he wanted and Quilla found his ideas exciting and racked her brains over ways and means of achieving the desired end result.

They bought tools, scratched their heads over where and how to begin to turn a mass of weeds and straggly fruit bushes into a picture-book cottage garden.

Fraser's energy was unbelievable and she did her best to keep up with him, and on the evenings when they found a gardening programme on the television they were there, glued to the set.

And at uncomplicated times like these she was hopeful for the future. She loved him desperately and perhaps, in time, he would learn how to love.

Besides, she was a fighter, wasn't she? She would make him love her. The time would come when she would no longer catch him looking at her with cold hard eyes, a cynical half-smile on his mouth. And sometimes when he looked at her there was no expression there at all, just a poker player's mask. And that, if anything, was worse.

In the middle of their second week at Old Ford they heard the phone ring from inside the cottage and they stopped what they were doing and stared at each other. It was the first time their honeymoon had been interrupted by someone from the outside world.

'I'll get it.' Fraser dropped the rake he'd been using and dusted down his hands, a frown between his eyes.

Quilla, straightening, instructed, 'When you come out, bring the jug of lemonade we made out of the fridge. I'm parched,' and watched him stride away, his earth-stained jeans riding low on his hips, the upper part of his magnificent body naked, tanned by the sun.

Smiling softly, she picked up the rake he'd been using and carried on where he'd left off. They'd finally hit a brainwave, hiring a man from the nearest village to rotovate the entire acre, the area to be cultivated. And from early morning Fraser had been raking the ground, Quilla picking out the more pernicious weed roots, carrying them in a bucket to the bonfire. It promised to be a long hard job, backbreaking, but they'd get there in the end, had plans to get lawn areas seeded in the autumn, the flowerbeds, paths and rockery area marked out.

For the next twelve months they would only use the cottage at weekends, spending the rest of the time in Belgravia. He hadn't said, but she knew he hoped that by this time next year there would be a child on the way. When they had a family he would want to live here permanently.

And that didn't bother her. Much as she loved the city, she preferred the cottage, the freedom and space, and Old Ford would be ideal for children.

Her womb stirred every time she thought of holding Fraser's child in her arms and she now knew what Marian must have gone through when she'd believed she would never conceive.

'We're going to have to go back to town.'

She had been so engrossed in her thoughts, in what she was doing, that she hadn't heard him approach, and she turned, leaning on the rake, watching his absorption as he balanced the jug of lemonade, two glasses, on a tray.

'Something cropped up?' She wiped her forearm over her perspiring brow and stripped off her heavy-duty gardening gloves before taking the tray from him.

'You can say that again.' He sat down on the upturned bucket and accepted the drink she gave him. 'My partners are of the opinion that it's something only I can handle.' His voice was dry, but she knew better then to question him. He didn't talk to her about his work. It was as if he kept her in a separate compartment from the rest of his life.

'Then I'd better go and pack.' She had finished her own drink and looked up to find his eyes on her. They were dark with regret and she knew he disliked having to leave as much as she did.

He said, 'I'm sorry about this. Do you mind too much?'

However much she minded it wouldn't make a scrap of difference. If he was needed he would go, his work would come first.

So she smiled and said, 'No, not at all.'

But he added, 'You could always stay on here. I won't be able to spend any time with you once we're back in town, not even in the evenings. So you could stay here, relax, and I'd be able to join you for the weekend.'

His eyes were intent on her face, as if for some reason her reply would tell him something about her, clarify something inside his head. She didn't know what. She only knew that, where he was, she wanted to be. Even if she saw very little of him he would, she assumed, come home to sleep. Since their marriage she couldn't imagine sleeping without him.

But she could hardly tell him that. He would pull the shutters up again. She had tried, tentatively, on more than one occasion, to let him know how she felt about him. But as soon as her conversation, the words she'd whispered during their more intimate moments, had touched on the romantic, he had invariably made some cynical reply, verbally splashing cold water over her, making her feel a fool.

And so she had stopped trying, prepared to take their relationship one slow step at a time. And now she answered, 'I'd rather go back to town. I can find plenty to do to keep me amused.'

He shot her a dark look, a look that said, I bet you can! and returned his glass to the tray with unnecessary force, then stood up, his back towards her, gathering up the tools they'd been using.

And yet again she felt the door closing on her, shutting her out in the cold, and sighed, walking back into the cottage to pack their things, leaving everything as they had found it, nothing to say they had ever been here at all.

* * *

She was going to have to find the time to tell Fraser that, despite anything he said, any threats he made, she was returning to work next week.

Find the courage, too!

They had been back in the city for less than thirty-six hours and already she felt silly with boredom. Maggie ran the Belgravia house with stream-lined efficiency, and had offered a polite but firm negative when Quilla had practically begged to be allowed to help.

She hadn't the temperament to live in idle luxury and, almost, she wished she had stayed at the cottage. And she knew what Fraser had meant when he'd said that his London house had never been a home. It was beautiful but sterile and she could well understand his excitement when he'd found Old Ford, known it could become the home he'd never really had.

If Fraser had his way she would never have anything more to do with Nico; he had an entrenched and misguided view of the relationship between them. But, apart from her love of her work, the time and money she had put in to making the business the success it was, her need to be kept busy and interested, she knew she couldn't let Nico down. The new girl would eventually be capable of taking her place, but not yet.

So tonight she would tell him. If, like last night, he again came home at around midnight, wound up from a gruelling day of meetings, long hours spent alone in the office afterwards, wanting only, so he had said, a stiff drink and bed, she would have to nerve herself to break the news.

She picked up a magazine and put it down again, wondering what to do with herself. She had made

an appointment to see her solicitor to deed her share
of Marshbrook to Marian, but her appointment
wasn't until tomorrow and the day stretched ahead,
empty and long. To make matters worse, it was
raining.

So the sound of the phone was a welcome distraction, and Jon said, 'Mari told me Fraser was
back in harness. So I guessed you'd be back in
town, too. It seems ages since we got together and
I'm bursting to tell you our news. How about
lunch? Somewhere a bit up-market to celebrate.'

It was good to hear his voice, and lunching with
him would break her day up, pass the time
pleasantly. She said, 'I'd love to. What are you
celebrating?'

'Mari's expecting a baby.' He sounded awe-
struck. 'The results came through yesterday.'

'That's wonderful!' Quilla could hardly believe
it. It seemed no time since her sister-in-law had been
visiting that clinic, secretly in despair because she
believed she couldn't conceive, that Jon didn't love
her anyway. 'I can't believe it's happened so
quickly!'

'Neither can we,' Jon chuckled elatedly. 'The
specialist was spot on. She only needed to relax,
stop getting so uptight. And when I'd managed to
convince the little idiot that I was as crazy about
her now as on the day I married her, and promised
to go and have tests myself if nothing happened
within a few months, she did just that. And bingo!'

After arranging where and when to meet, Quilla
found Maggie, told her she wouldn't be in for lunch,
and ran upstairs to get changed. She would have
time before meeting Jon to go to the baby de-
partment at Harrods. Early days yet, of course, and

she wouldn't buy anything. But she could look, couldn't she?

Even so, as she was shown to the table where her brother was waiting, she was clutching a carrier and she laid out the tiny white bootees threaded with white silk ribbon, the matching little jacket and cap, and grinned when Jon's face went red with pride.

'I just couldn't resist them,' she explained, packing them away and accepting the menu from an amused waiter's hand. 'You wouldn't think any baby would be small enough to fit into those tiny things.'

'You're looking great.' Jon changed the subject quickly, covered in typical male embarrassment. 'Married life obviously agrees with you.'

She was wearing a structured cream-coloured suit, an amber blouse, her hair pinned up in a sophisticated style in honour of her surroundings. The work in the fresh air, the sun, had given her normally pale skin a healthy glow, so she supposed she was looking as if everything was coming up roses.

That her husband didn't love her, that their marriage had been forced, his obsession with her pushing him to threaten her with her brother's ruin as the only means of getting his own way, was something she could never tell anyone. Least of all Jon. He would blame himself. If he hadn't begged her to step in and try to lure Fraser away from his wife, then they would never have met.

The thought of never having met him made Quilla go cold. Their marriage was far from perfect but she couldn't imagine life without him.

Pushing her own problems aside, she concentrated on the menu, gave her order then sipped her martini, her eyes smiling at Jon over the rim of her glass. He made his selection from the wine-list and passed it back to the waiter, then leaned forward, his elbows on the table, telling her,

'I've been dying to know—what was that business with the finance agreement about?'

Quilla's heart missed a beat. Had Fraser pulled something devious? Much as she loved him, she had to admit he was a tricky devil. The document he and Jon had signed with such ostentation could have been a blind. Was the new development still being held up for lack of funds?

She put her glass down carefully on the table and made her voice light, her words casual. 'What are you talking about?'

'Oh, come off it!' he chided affectionately. 'At lunch, after the ceremony. Fraser had primed me beforehand, of course. I was bursting with curiosity but when McGill commands the likes of me obey, no questions asked! I was to sign a copy of the agreement and look suitably gratified. Bloody crazy, if you ask me!'

'You mean Kent Construction still hasn't got the backing for the south coast development?' Quilla asked through frozen lips. She would never forgive the bastard for this. Never!

Jon leaned back as their first course was brought to the table and Quilla looked down at the prawn doria she'd ordered and felt ill. And then he laughed, squeezing lemon juice over his smoked salmon, shaking his head.

'I don't know what gives you that idea. The funds were made available weeks ago—when you were away with the French collection.' He met her wide, puzzled eyes with a shrug. 'That's why I couldn't understand why he'd dug up that copy, asked me to sign it all over again. The original was water-tight, the firm's solicitors saw to that.'

Quilla couldn't begin to understand what was going on and she said slowly, picking her words carefully, unable to tell him the whole truth, 'After I got back from Rome I tried to contact you at the office. I didn't know you were away. I spoke to Roger Campbell, mentioned the south coast project, and he said you were still waiting for the go-ahead. I took that to mean the funding.'

For a moment Jon looked puzzled and then he grinned. 'Oh, that. There'd been a slight planning hiccup, but it eventually got sorted. And now it's all systems go. But that still doesn't explain the farce with the copy.'

'A private joke,' Quilla invented rapidly. 'Fraser was humouring me. Let's leave it, shall we?' She began, belatedly, to eat. 'I'd rather talk about the baby—how long is Mari going to carry on at work? And what do you want, a boy or a girl?'

The subject kept Jon occupied and, while appearing to give him all her attention, her mind was working furiously.

On each occasion Fraser had blackmailed her, he'd had no leverage. In the first instance he had never had an affair with her sister-in-law and in the second he had already made the funds Jon needed available. There had been no question at all of his ruining Kent Construction.

That made him doubly devious. But oh, so human. He must have wanted her a great deal to go to such lengths, making empty threats because he could see no other way, knowing that the truth could easily be discovered. He must indeed have wanted her, not only in his bed but as his wife.

She felt almost delirious with hope. He wasn't the utterly ruthless bastard she had believed him to be. He was clever and tricky, calmly using the double bluff, but never callous and ruthless. He would never deliberately set out to harm.

And he'd wanted her enough to put himself right on the line, knowing that she only had to question Marian, or Jon, to reveal the emptiness of his threats. And from such need, surely love could grow?

It might take years, but she was willing to wait. And hope. And now, as far as she was concerned, the past was dead, their future, as husband and wife, a clean slate.

'And it will be nice to see a pony in the paddock again.' Jon had leapt far ahead of her—the unborn child was already around five or six years old!

Quilla blinked and smiled. Time enough to think of Fraser later, when she was alone, waiting for him to come home tonight. They were going to have to clear the air, once and for all, get rid of any lingering doubts and misconceptions. And one of the first things to make him realise was her lack of any romantic involvement with Nico French!

But for now she must give her whole attention to her brother and for the remainder of the meal she managed it, feeling more light-hearted and hopeful than she had for months.

Then, refusing more coffee, she leaned back in her seat, glancing around the room. The restaurant was fairly crowded, full of beautiful people, some of the faces famous, and her eyes widened as she saw Merla Raines enter with a flurry.

The model looked as stunning as ever, sexy perfection wrapped up in an outrageously daring red dress, her scarlet lips stretched wide, revealing dazzling white teeth as she scanned the room to see and be seen.

The head waiter appeared as if by magic, but his deferential half-bow wasn't for Merla. It was for her escort, for Fraser McGill!

Quilla closed her eyes on a wave of shock and nausea, unable to believe what she'd seen. But when she opened them again nothing had changed and she had to believe it.

And the stabbing pain of jealousy was so intense that it took her breath away and she wanted to hide. Anything to get away from the evidence of her own eyes.

The last time she'd seen the model—vulgarly known in high fashion circles as Merla the Maneater—they'd been in Rome, and Fraser had put in an appearance, and Merla had made it patently clear that she thought he'd make a very tasty morsel indeed!

True, Fraser hadn't taken her up on her blatant offer, but only because he'd had unfinished business with her, Quilla. His ego had demanded some kind of retribution for the way she had turned him down. He'd wanted her and he'd made good and sure he got her, and, having satisfied his obsession, got it under control, he was taking up the sexy model's earlier offer with both hands!

The couple were being shown to a table and Merla was practically draped all over him, one of her heavily ringed hands possessively clutching his as it lay on her bared shoulder, and she saw Fraser bend his head to hers, his sensual mouth softening in the look she knew so well. She dragged in her breath on an upsurge of pain.

'Are you all right?' Jon had obviously noticed her distress. He was frowning. 'You've gone white.'

'I'm fine,' she assured him quickly, a wooden smile pinned to her face. At least he hadn't seen Merla and Fraser practically drooling all over each other. She wouldn't have been able to stand the humiliation if he had.

'Good.' Jon still wasn't convinced. 'For a moment I thought you were going to faint.'

'Probably the heat.' How was she going to be able to stand, walk out of here, without disgracing herself completely? Her legs felt like water.

And Jon said, 'Yes, probably,' although they both knew it was cool and rainy outside, just pleasantly warm in here.

Thankfully, he was still concerned enough about her to give her his undivided attention as he escorted her out on to the street. He hadn't noticed her husband and the sexy model deep in animated conversation at their table. And she didn't object when he put her into a taxi, his eyes very serious as he told her to take care.

At least someone cared about her, she thought drearily as she let herself into the house.

Tightening her lips and squaring her shoulders, she went up to the room she had shared with Fraser last night. She would change, go for a walk in the rain, come to terms with life.

She had her brother and Marian, she had Nico, the house in Southwark and her job. She had a lot going for her.

But she didn't have a husband. She could live with the knowledge that he didn't love her because there had always been the hope that he would change, learn to love her. But she couldn't live with him knowing that his former womanising habits were unchanged, never knowing who he was seeing, whose bed he was sharing.

As far as she was concerned, her marriage was over.

CHAPTER TEN

'WELL of course you can stay, there's no question. But what the hell——?'

'Don't ask,' Quilla said, her voice terse. Nico hadn't been able to believe his eyes when she'd walked through the front door only minutes ago, dragging her suitcase. And he still couldn't believe she'd walked in for good, even though he stood in her bedroom doorway, watching as she unpacked her things.

She had no intention of telling anyone why she had run out on McGill, that was her business. The marriage was over, that was all anyone needed to know.

Walking in the rain until long after the street-lamps had come on, their light reflected on the shining wet pavements, had purged her system of the sickening jealous fury that had threatened to tear her apart, leaving her calm, knowing what she had to do, in control of her own destiny again.

Once back in the house in Belgravia it had only taken her moments to re-pack her case, leaving a note for Fraser, curt and to the point, telling him she was going, wouldn't be back, warning him against trying to use his usual brand of persuasive threats, making it all sound very final.

And now it was gone eleven and it was going to be a long night. Her mind was too icy and clear to allow her to relax, to lose the trauma of the day in sleep.

'There's only one thing,' Nico looked out of his depth, his usual panache deserting him in the face of what he guessed was some kind of emergency. 'Pam's been working full time while you've been away. She's shaping up pretty well, and when she told me she'd been having words with the girl she shares with I, well, I suggested she moved in here. I didn't know you'd be coming back.'

And neither had anyone else, Quilla thought sourly. She and Fraser had been married for under two weeks and it was already over. But she said crisply, 'Don't panic. There's room enough for all of us, provided Pam's willing to sleep in the box-room. We can dock the rent out of her salary.'

'You could move into my bed, anytime,' Nico said thickly, and Quilla went still with shock. Maybe Fraser had been right, maybe he'd picked up on something she'd never noticed in all the years she'd worked with Nico. Maybe the platonic relationship had been anything but, inside Nico's head. Maybe her abortive marriage to Fraser had acted as a catalyst.

Any thoughts poor Nico had in that direction had to be squashed, so she said, her voice firm and crisp, 'I don't think so, thank you,' and snapped the lid of her suitcase back in place.

She had done all the unpacking she needed to do and the way Nico was hovering got on her nerves. When he suggested, 'How about a nightcap to help you relax?' she had to count ten before answering to stop herself biting his head off.

None of this mess was Nico's fault. He had always been a good friend to her and, despite his earlier revealing remark, she was going to have to work with him for the foreseeable future and pretend, for both their sakes, that nothing had changed. Besides, it wouldn't be fair or reasonable to make him suffer because she'd been fool enough to fall in love with a two-timing, conscienceless bastard. So she dredged up a smile and said, 'I'd like that. Give me a moment and I'll join you downstairs.'

As the door closed behind him she faced the mirror. No wonder Nico had looked dumbfounded; she looked a wreck. Her hair was plastered to her skull, hanging below her shoulders in rats' tails, the jeans and jacket she'd put on before taking that walk soaked through with London rain. She had to get herself together physically as well as mentally, the one was as important as the other.

It took only ten minutes to shower, rough-dry her hair and rub moisturiser into her skin. It was far too late to dress and so she wrapped herself in a thick towelling robe and went down to join Nico, who might be reduced to thinking she'd done another moonlight flit.

He'd switched on the electric fire because the night was cold and there was only a single table-lamp burning, adding to the cosy, intimate effect. And he must have been on tenterhooks, waiting for her, because as soon as she walked into the room she saw him relax.

'Drink this.' He put a glass into her hand, steered her to one of the sofas and sat down beside her, his one glass on the table in front of them.

She looked at the huge measure of whisky he'd given her and frowned. When he'd mentioned a nightcap she'd been thinking in terms of hot milk or chocolate. But, what the hell, the spirit would probably knock her out far more effectively than an innocuous hot drink. She took a mouthful and shuddered as it burned its way down her throat and Nico said, 'That's better. You looked as though you were in shock. Are you going to tell me what this is all about?'

'No.' Her tone was mild but the answer was un-equivocal. No one but she knew the truth about her short and traumatic marriage and no one ever would. Fraser hadn't married her for love, far from it. He'd married her because, like his father before him, he needed a mother for his heir, a wife he would never have any reason to be ashamed of.

The only emotion involved, as far as he had been concerned, had been lust. And, unlike the other women he'd been involved with, he hadn't been able to get her into his bed and so, needing a wife at some stage of his life, he had settled on her.

And the element of revenge had come into it, too, adding an extra purpose, mending his hurt ego. She had turned down his offer once and he had been determined she wouldn't get the chance to do it twice.

But she'd known that all along, not seeing it quite as clearly as she did now, but guessing it. But always, foolishly, hoping. Hoping he would learn to love her, never dreaming he would continue to take mistresses whenever he felt like it.

For the sake of her love for him she could have borne many things. But not that. Never that. Given his track record where the female sex was concerned, his self-admitted inability to love—which equated with an inability to stay faithful to one woman—she didn't have to be a genius to know that if Fraser weren't Merla's lover at the moment then he very soon would be.

The model had been heard to boast quite openly, as if it were something to be proud of, that she could get any man she fancied, and had gone on to prove it, time after time. And if the man she fancied happened to be already married, well—tough on the wife! And after Merla there would be others, and that was something Quilla couldn't live with.

'Well, that's up to you, of course. But if you ever want to talk about it, get it off your chest, I'll always be here. We've been friends for a long time.' Nico got up to replenish his glass and Quilla stared into the remaining amber liquid in hers, hoping he wasn't hurt by her refusal to confide in him. But she couldn't. It was far too painful and, even if she'd wanted to bare her soul to him she knew, after his invitation to take her to his bed she had to tread carefully, keep him firmly at arm's length.

And then the doorbell pealed long and insistently and Quilla froze. The sound was wild, untamed, in the quiet room. She knew it was Fraser, and Nico said crossly, 'Who the hell's that? It's almost midnight, for Pete's sake!'

'Don't answer it,' she pleaded through stiff lips, her face very white.

But the sound of fists against the door was worse then the persistent ringing of the bell and Nico swore, 'God! Whoever it is will have the door down!' and stamped out of the room in a temper. Quilla began to shake, wrapping her arms around her body, wishing the floor would open up so that she could dive in and pull the carpet over her head.

'Someone for you, dear one,' Nico said edgily from the doorway, and she flung him a frightened look as Fraser pushed past him into the room, his hard eyes taking in her state of undress, the two whisky glasses on the table.

He was wearing an immaculate business suit, dark grey with a lighter, very faint pinstripe, and he looked as if he would like to kill her, the cold rage coming off him in waves, filling the room with ice.

'Please leave us,' he said to Nico, keeping his eyes on Quilla.

Nico, after one look at Quilla's terrified face, blustered, 'Hang on, there. This is my house. Mine and Quilla's. You can't tell me what to do in it.'

It would be no use, she knew it wouldn't. And it wasn't. And she bowed to the inevitable, not blaming Nico because no one but a suicidal fool would tangle with a man with murder on his face.

'Get out.' He didn't have to raise his voice, to threaten.

The look in his eyes did everything necessary, and Nico edged out of the doorway, his apologetic, 'Just shout if you need me,' doing nothing at all to reassure her.

For a long time he said nothing, just looked at her, his eyes cold. And then, when she could stand no more of this particular brand of torture, she bit out, 'Didn't you read my letter?'

He dipped his head. 'That's why I'm here. Did you really think I'd let you walk out on me, come back to him, and sit back quietly and take it?'

She hadn't thought of it that way. Her letter had said it all, but she hadn't taken his pride, his possessiveness into full consideration.

He moved then, away from the door, coming towards her, and his mouth was a cruel line as he rapped out, 'Nice set-up. Comfortable sofa, soft lights, plenty of booze. And I'd lay odds you're not wearing anything at all under that robe.'

She wasn't going to argue with him—what was the point? He wouldn't believe her, whatever she said. But when he sat beside her she edged frantically to her feet, wincing as he grasped her wrist and pulled her down again.

'Stay where I can keep you under control,' he instructed coldly. 'And you needn't worry, I'm not going to touch you.'

'Why? Satiated?' She should have held her tongue, but the words had come out instinctively, voicing her hurt, and he gave her a level look, his mouth thinning.

'What's that supposed to mean?'

'If you can't guess I'm not about to tell you,' she snapped, her own temper rising now. How dared he come here and harass her? Sitting too close. She knew every inch of the superb male body beneath those expensively tailored clothes, knew every line and plane of his face better than she knew her own. But she had cut him out of her life and having him close, this close, was a torment she wasn't ready to face.

'Don't play games with me, I'm not in the mood,' he said with a bite. 'Coming home to find you'd gone back to your lover isn't my idea of a picnic after the kind of day I've had.'

'Hard work, was she?' she snapped right back, furious with him. The urgent summons back to the bank had been no such thing. Just dear little Merla phoning to let him know she was back in England and available. No wonder he had suggested she stay on at the cottage, no wonder 'business' kept him out late at night. If she hadn't insisted on returning to town with him he probably wouldn't have gone near the house in Belgravia!

He could lie and cheat, make no commitment, expecting her to stay quietly at home, ask no questions. If she hadn't loved him she might have been able to put up with it. Loving him, she could do no such thing.

'I don't know what you mean.' His voice was flat and, for the first time, she noticed the shadows under his eyes, the lines of strain on his face. She turned away quickly; why should she care if he looked near the end of his tether? He had brought it on himself.

And he was sitting too close. His nearness made every last millimetre of her skin feel unbearably sensitised, and she edged away, but he caught her wrist and hauled her back, his face running with angry colour as he ground out, 'Just tell me why you left me to come back to him. He must be fantastic in bed.'

'I wouldn't know,' Quilla spat back, her eyes glittering. She was sick of the games they were playing, sick of him, of everything.

The pressure of his hand increased, crushing her bones, his voice a cool sneer as he asked, 'Are you trying to tell me you've never had an affair with him?' looking deep into her eyes, his face only inches away.

His mouth was so near, the straight line of his lips predatory, and she felt her own begin to quiver and bit down hard on the tender flesh, her voice oddly thick as she told him wearily, 'I've tried before. But you get an idea in your head and you won't let go of it.'

'Only because you put it there in the first place,' he pointed out.

'You were trying to make me agree to be your mistress,' she reminded him tartly. 'I let you think Nico was my lover to put you off. And if you don't believe me, call him down and ask. I came back here because I own half the house, half the business, and, married to you or not, I intend to go on working. I always did—even when I stupidly thought the marriage could work, I meant to keep my job. And let go of me, you're hurting!'

Immediately, the punishing grip of his fingers eased and she snatched her hand away, rubbing the reddened skin, her eyes accusing, and he asked levelly, a slight frown pulling his brows together, 'You've lived with him for four years, you can't deny that.'

'Shared a house,' she corrected snappily. 'There is a difference. We bought it between us, my office is here and so is his studio. It made good business sense,' and saw the sudden flicker of acceptance in his eyes, of belief, and knew the victory was hollow because whether he believed her or not didn't matter.

Nothing could change the fact that he'd lied to her about needing to come back to town on business, taking up what must have been the open-ended invitation Merla had made in Rome. She needed men like a plant needed water and McGill's track record when it came to accepting invitations of that kind was legendary.

She had seen them together with her own eyes, practically wrapped around each other, her husband too absorbed in his new conquest to notice her!

He had his arm along the back of the sofa now, slightly more relaxed. She couldn't say the same for herself. He was making her feel appallingly edgy. And his eyes held an expression she couldn't read as he said, 'I can accept your need to continue working—I'm not the complete chauvinist. It was the idea of your having anything to do with wonder boy that stuck in my throat. But if you're not in love with Nico French, if he's nothing more than a friend and business partner, why did you walk out on me?'

She picked up her whisky glass for something to do, swirling the contents round, looking at them. She couldn't look at him.

Telling him she had seen him with Merla Raines at lunchtime, drooling over each other, when he was supposed to be working flat out on some crisis concerned with the bank, would be too revealing. She couldn't stay married to him, spend the rest of her life wondering who his new lady was. But to tell him would let him know how much she cared, that she loved him. She had too much pride. So she said gruffly, 'You can't force me to stay with you,' and saw his eyes darken.

'It was never my intention to force you to stay,' he replied bleakly, the muscles on his face tightening, pulling the flesh back against the rugged bones. And she got jerkily to her feet, walking across to the other side of the room, pulling aside one of the curtains to stare out into the dark wet streets, the pool of yellow lamplight illuminating the Lotus parked outside. He was either a congenital liar or he'd lost his memory. He had forced her through every stage of their stormy relationship!

'I'd hoped that in time I could make you want to stay. Need me enough to trust your life and happiness to me.'

He had come to stand behind her, very close, and her body went rigid, her throat closing up, hurting. He could smooth talk his way out of any corner, make a woman believe anything.

But not this woman. She said thickly, 'If that's what you want you should learn to tame your appetite. Even in a loveless marriage there has to room for respect and fidelity,' and felt his hands on her shoulders, burning her through the thick fabric.

'And if I knew what you were talking about I might be able to think straight.'

She heard pain in his voice, like the pain of a man who had never known defeat before. And his head, as he laid it against hers, was heavy, and the lump in her throat grew as she tried to think how to answer him. He was fine in so many ways and it saddened her to know that he would never be able to trust his love to anyone.

Perhaps bluntness was the best way, the quickest, cleanest way to end it all. And she said drearily, 'I saw you with Merla Raines today. I'm amazed you could find time to take her to lunch, considering the crisis at the bank that forced you to abandon our honeymoon. I dare say, knowing Merla of old, and recalling how smitten you seemed when you met her in Rome, that she made you an offer you couldn't refuse. And that's fine. If that's the way you want to conduct your life, fine. But don't expect me to be a part of it.'

His whole body had gone very still, and somehow she was leaning back against him. She could feel the heavy beat of his heart, feel the fevered male heat of him. She didn't want that, despite all that had happened she couldn't trust herself when he was this close, and she pulled away from him but his arms came round her, tightening, his voice ragged as he groaned, 'How can you be so stupid? Do you find it that difficult to trust me? There was a crisis, your sister-in-law will be able to verify that if you can't bring yourself to believe me. But it wasn't as bad as it had initially seemed. And having steered us out of it, apart from a few loose ends I stayed on last night and tonight to tie up, I was free to give lunch to one of our notable clients, a certain American billionaire—a duty thing.'

She felt his hands tighten briefly on her shoulders before he moved away from her, and she turned to watch him pace the room, restless, like a caged tiger.

'Just before I was due to meet him his secretary phoned through. He'd been detained, but would meet me at the restaurant in about half an hour. Only there was a slight problem. His companion would be already on her way, the lady had spent the morning shopping, and he, the secretary, had no way of contacting her. So would I entertain the lady until our client arrived? It was the first time I heard of the extra guest.' He pulled a face. 'But our wealthy American friend is nothing if not unconventional. And I couldn't believe my eyes when I met Merla getting out of a taxi outside the restaurant.'

Quilla shot him a frantic look. Could he possibly be telling the truth? Something in his voice, his whole demeanour, told her he was, and she moistened her lips and queried, 'So Merla's found herself a bottomless pocket book?'

Fraser smiled thinly. 'Until she's extracted as much as she can she'll blinker herself as far as other men are concerned. She likes the male sex, the richer the better. She's engagingly open about her little weaknesses, and can be almost embarrassingly affectionate. And before you start accusing me of indulging in a one-night stand with her in Rome, I'll put the record straight. She introduced herself to me, not the other way round. I couldn't get rid of her. And as that crowd of yours were dining in the hotel I tagged along. There's safety in numbers. And our friend Merla drank too much; she was practically falling over. One of your dressers told me it was because she could see she wasn't getting anywhere with me. I was too mad about your sneaky departure with Nico French, wondering what you were doing and where you were doing it, to pay any attention to any other woman. Since I met you no other woman has existed.'

She had to fight the almost overwhelming need to believe that statement, so she snapped defiantly, 'No? What about the blonde who made it to the gossip columns with you? They said she was your constant companion. Or was she simply a figment of someone's imagination?'

'She existed,' he said heavily. He had stopped pacing, his hands thrust into the pockets of his trousers, the line of his shoulders weary. 'You'd come into my life like a thunderbolt. I didn't know what had hit me. And at every stage you held me off. I was getting out of my depth for the first time in my life and it scared me silly. So I tried to put you right out of my mind. But dating Belinda got me nowhere. I simply couldn't see her—all I could see, think of, dream of, was you. I came to Rome to tell you how I felt and you showed me the door, made it painfully clear that you preferred Nico. And so I plotted and schemed to make you marry me. And that got me nowhere, either. I never wanted to trap you, I only ever wanted to love you, to make you return that love one day.' He gave her a long, bleak look. 'I'm sorry. Trying to capture a dream, cage it, was the worst mistake I've ever made.' His face expressionless, he turned to the door. 'I won't trouble you again. I won't say I'm happy about it, but you have your freedom. Get your solicitor to contact mine.'

And was gone. She heard his heavy footsteps in the hall and came out of shock with a jolt and ran after him, the long skirts of her robe flying around her legs.

He was just closing the front door behind him and she didn't know if she'd heard him right or whether she'd been simply hearing things she wanted to hear. But she had to find out, and she jerked the door open and called with thick urgency, 'Come back, Fraser.'

She saw him stiffen and thought he would ignore her, but he turned slowly, his face shuttered, and walked back towards the house. It had stopped raining but the night air was cool and she drew the edges of her robe together at her throat, shivering. And he looked down at her, frowning.

'Whatever it is, couldn't it wait?'

She grabbed his sleeve, pulling him back inside the house, slamming the door back in place with her foot. 'You said you loved me. Did you mean it?' she challenged, and saw pain darken his eyes, just for a moment, before he was back in control, enquiring blandly,

'What do you think?'

'You told me you didn't know the meaning of love, that it was just a pretty word,' she answered him shakily, her foolish heart plummeting because she must have been hearing things after all.

And he said tightly, his teeth clenched, 'Then I was mistaken, wasn't I? I've been mistaken over too many things as far as you're concerned.' Their eyes met and she felt her heart begin to thump. She saw the lines of pain etched starkly around his beautiful, sensual mouth and could have wept for them both as he said thickly, 'Of course I love you. How could you not have known it? I told you things about myself, my family, I've never told another living soul. I took you to Old Ford to get your re-action to what, until then, had been my secret place. Because, although I didn't know it at the time, I wanted you there, as my wife, with my children. I don't wear my heart on my sleeve, Quilla, but I laid everything on the line for you, who I am, what I am, what makes me tick. How could you not have known?'

He was in mental agony. She knew he was baring his soul as he had never done before, and she felt her love for him grow, deepen, until it filled every part of her, and she moved closer to him, winding her arms around his neck, feeling him stiffen defensively at the contact. She whispered,

'Because you didn't tell me.'

'How could I?' he asked huskily as she put her lips against the stubbled darkness of his jaw. 'I didn't know myself until you turned down my suggestion of an affair and told me you preferred Nico French. I was eaten alive with jealousy. Up until then all I'd thought about was wanting you. I thought that wanting was all it was. Again, I was wrong. When you walked out of that hotel with the man I thought was your lover the truth hit me like a ton of bricks. I loved you and had to have the chance to make you love me. And I made the chance, regardless of the price I had to pay.'

He made to put her aside but she clung, her hands going up to tangle in the thick darkness of his hair, pulling his head down until his lips were a whisper away from hers, and she felt him shudder, felt her own answering response leap to shattering life before she got out throatily, 'Loving me, as I love you, is the only price you're going to have to pay. But you'll be paying it for the rest of your life, or I'll know the reason why!'

She felt the quiver run through his tautly held body, heard the thread of hope in his voice as he demanded, 'Say that again. About loving me.'

She complied very gladly, shuddering with ecstasy as he buried his mouth in the scented skin at the base of her throat, and, her head held back she gasped with delight as his lips moved downwards, nuzzling aside the edges of the thick robe, managing to tell him, 'I think I've loved you since I first saw you. But I didn't know it, either, until you took me to Old Ford as your wife. I didn't tell you, because I didn't think you knew how to love. I just loved on hope. But I'll tell you every day of my life for as long as I live.'

And Fraser muttered thickly, 'Come home, now, my darling. Come back with me.'

And she murmured, 'Please, oh, yes, please.'

Behind them Nico said snappily, 'Don't mind me! I heard the door slam. I thought, "Oh, goody, they've gone, one or both of them!" And down I trot, overcome with relief, and here you still are. Frolicking!'

His voice had gone very dry and Quilla giggled, feeling the answering ripple of amusement pass through Fraser's body, and Nico swept past them, his nose in the air.

'Let me know if you'll still be here for breakfast— one likes to have a vague idea.'

'Shove off, French!' Fraser grinned down into Quilla's sparkling eyes. 'We're on our way, and don't worry, you won't be losing your business partner, but be prepared to have me poking my nose in. As my wife's financial adviser I'll be keeping a very close eye on all her assets, believe me,' and scooped her up into his arms, hovering while she opened the door with one hand and clasped the other round his neck.

And Nico screeched, putting on an act, camping it up to hide the reality of his feelings, 'You can't take her like that! What about her clothes?'

'Try to stop me,' Fraser replied good-humouredly. 'My wife will be back for her things on Monday morning when she turns up for work. In the meantime, I don't think she'll feel the lack.'

And she wouldn't. She knew enough about this much-loved husband of hers to know she wouldn't feel the lack at all.

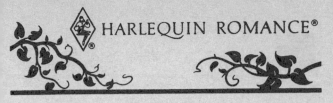

HARLEQUIN ROMANCE®

welcomes you

BACK TO THE RANCH

Let your favorite Romance authors take you West!

Authors like Susan Fox, Debbie Macomber, Roz Denny, Rebecca Winters and more!

Let them introduce you to wonderful women and strong, sexy men—the men of the West. Ranchers and horsemen and cowboys and lawmen...

Beginning in June 1993

Wherever Harlequin books are sold.

HARLEQUIN ROMANCE®

HARLEQUIN PRESENTS®

A Year DOWN UNDER

In 1993, Harlequin Presents celebrates the land down under. In May, let us take you to Auckland, New Zealand, in SECRET ADMIRER by Susan Napier, Harlequin Presents #1554.

Scott Gregory is ready to make his move. He's realized Grace is a novice at business *and* emotionally vulnerable— a young widow struggling to save her late husband's company. But Grace is a fighter. She's taking business courses and she's determined not to forget Scott's reputation as a womanizer. Even if it means adding another battle to the war—a fight against her growing attraction to the handsome New Zealander!

Share the adventure—and the romance— of A Year Down Under!

Available this month in
A YEAR DOWN UNDER

A DANGEROUS LOVER
by Lindsay Armstrong
Harlequin Presents #1546
Wherever Harlequin books are sold.